MONEY

money

THE KEATYN CHRONICLES: BOOK 10

JILLIAN DODD

Jillian Dodd Inc.
N. Redington Beach, FL

ISBN: 978-1-940652-74-0

THIS BOOK IS FOR
those like me who enjoy
trashy reality TV.

Books by Jillian Dodd

The Keatyn Chronicles
USA TODAY bestselling young adult contemporary romance set in
an East Coast boarding school.
Stalk Me
Kiss Me
Date Me
Love Me
Adore Me
Hate Me
Get Me
Fame
Power
Money
Sex
Love

Keatyn Unscripted
Aiden

That Boy Series
Small-town contemporary romance series about falling in love with
the boy next door.
That Boy
That Wedding
That Baby
That Divorce

The Love Series
Contemporary, standalone romances following the very sexy
Crawford family.
Vegas Love
Broken Love
Fake Love

Spy Girl Series
Young adult romance series about a young spy who just might save
the world.
The Prince
The Eagle
The Society
The Valiant

Jillian Dodd and Kenzie Harp
Young adult travel romance.
Girl off the Grid

SUNDAY, OCTOBER 12TH
ASHER VINEYARDS – SONOMA COUNTY
Ariela

I'M LYING ACROSS my bed talking to Riley on the phone like I used to do in high school.

He's in L.A. all week, and I'll be at the vineyard getting everything set for Keatyn and Aiden's wedding. We agreed to talk every night and decide at the wedding if we wanted to move forward with a relationship.

I already know I do.

I'm so glad we both ended up at Eastbrooke for homecoming. It's hard to believe that neither of us had ever been back.

Well, not that surprising for me but, I have to say, I was shocked he hadn't gone either.

For years, I've thought about—dreamed about—what I would say if I saw him there again, but the reality was better than I had imagined.

I feel like we can move forward now. Not forget the past, but get past it—if that makes sense.

And when Riley says, "I think that's what this weekend did for me. When we said goodbye, I started focusing on what could be—what, hopefully, *will* be—and not on what *should've* been," I feel even more hopeful, practically giddy.

"That's a big shift in mentality," I say, then hear a shrill voice calling out Riley's name.

"Shelby, what are you doing here?" Riley says. "I told you I didn't want to see you again."

I cringe when I hear the name Shelby. She's the girl who was in his penthouse wearing practically nothing when Riley and I went there after dancing at the club.

"I need to talk to you, Riley," she says. "It's important. Can I please come up?"

Um, no! I don't want her going anywhere with him! "Shelby, as in *naked, leather-strap, threesome Shelby*?" I ask, reminding Riley that I'm still on the phone.

"Uh, hang on," he says to me, doing something that muffles his conversation but still allows me to hear.

"Whatever you need to say, you can say here," Riley says to her.

"God, you're such an ass," she hisses loudly. "I thought you might want to do this in private."

"I don't want to do anything with you—in public or in private," he says, causing my heart to swell. He loves me. I know deep down in my heart that he still loves me.

And that's all that matters.

He told me he's been with a lot of women but only been serious with one. *Me.*

And I can handle it. I can be confident knowing

that I was the only one to ever have his heart, regardless of what others may have done with his body.

"Well, you're going to have to now, Riley," Shelby shrills. "Because I'm pr—"

BEEP. BEEP. BEEP. The call drops.

I quickly call back, but it goes straight to voicemail.

I pick up one of the menus I was reviewing before Riley called and double check it for accuracy, but I can't seem to concentrate because what I heard as the call ended keeps replaying in the back of my mind.

I'm pr—

I'm pr—

I'm pr—

Oh my God. Did she just tell him that she's *pregnant?*

RILEY'S PENTHOUSE - L.A.

I'M WEARING A huge smile as I get dropped off at my building and walk through the door, talking to Ariela on the phone.

Having her come back into my life after so many years has been both excruciating and exhilarating. But this weekend changed things. We faced our past together and, in one week, we're going to decide if we want to pursue a future together.

As much as I want to be with her, honestly, I'm a little torn about it.

Part of me wants nothing more than to pretend we never broke up. But the reality is that she's married. And even though she filed for a divorce, I wonder if it's too much too soon.

In a very short time—on a whim—she came to California, was reunited with me, slept with me, filed for a divorce, got a new job, and faced her demons at Eastbrooke. I mean, how many more life changes can she throw at herself all at once?

I loved her with everything I was in high school, and I was devastated when she left with nothing more than a goodbye.

And since she's come back, she's wreaked more havoc in my life.

Soon, I'll have to decide if I want to risk another relationship with her. Even though she still looks like the girl I loved, she's different—life, age, and time have that effect.

"Riley!" A shrill voice stops me in my tracks, wiping the smile off my face.

"Shelby, what are you doing here?" I ask, as she gets up from the couch in the lobby. "I told you I didn't want to see you again."

"I need to talk to you, Riley. It's important. Can I please come up?"

I know girls like her. No way I'm letting her come up.

Ever.

"Shelby, as in *naked, leather-strap, threesome Shelby?*" Ariela asks in my ear.

"Uh, hang on," I say to her, putting the phone against my chest. Then I say discreetly, "Shelby, whatever you need to say, you can say here."

"God, you're such an ass," she hisses loudly. "I thought you might want to do this in private."

"I don't want to do anything with you—in public or in private."

"Well, you're going to have to now, Riley. Because I'm pregnant," she says, uttering the words no man wants to hear from a three-night screw.

"You're *what?*"

"Do you really want to do this here?" she asks, glancing toward my doorman.

"Fine. Come up." I drag her into the elevator. Once it closes, I say, "I don't know who you've been fucking, but if you're pregnant, there's no way that it's mine."

"Yes, it is, Riley. I haven't been with anyone since we broke up."

"We didn't break up. You went to a few events with me. We fucked. And I used a condom every single time."

She shrugs. "I don't know what to tell you. They aren't one hundred percent effective. I'm sorry, Riley. I certainly didn't plan on getting pregnant."

"Aren't you on the pill?"

"No, it made me fat."

I shake my head. I can't fucking believe this. But I'm not stupid either. I go into my guest bathroom, grab a pregnancy test out of the cabinet, and then hand it to her. "Take this."

"Why do you have that?"

"Honey, you're not the first girl to tell me she's pregnant." I open it up and hand it to her. "Go pee on it, bring it out, and we'll watch. See what happens."

She hesitates, just as they all do. "Um, I don't know if it will work yet. I'm barely pregnant."

"So you didn't do a test?"

"Yes, I did a test, Riley. God, you're being such an ass."

She's right. I am. "I'm sorry. Please, for me, go take the test."

"I will, I'm just saying that they aren't all as accurate as the one I took." She lets out a dramatic sigh and goes into the bathroom, not bothering to shut the door. When she sees me watching her pee, she gives me a sexy smile.

I turn around.

Fuck.

Of course, *that's* what got me into this mess.

Please, please, don't let her be pregnant.

I hear the toilet flush and turn around.

"Here's the stick, Riley. I'm going to sit down. Pregnancy is exhausting."

She flops down on my couch while I stare at the stick, willing the line not to change.

But it does.

I sit down on the couch next to her, holding my head. "I can't fucking believe this."

She puts her hand on my thigh. "I know we weren't together very long, but we had a lot of fun. And, if I'm being honest, I like you a lot. No, that's a lie. I'm in love with you. If I had to get pregnant, I'm glad it's your baby. I think we should just make the best of it."

I nod. If I am the father of her baby, I need to be a man. A father. "I agree. We'll make the best of it."

She does a little bounce and smiles. "And we should get married right away. I don't want to wait until I'm showing. I saw the sexiest dress, daddy."

"Don't call me that."

"I'm sorry, but now you are one! So, it fits!" She wraps her arms around my neck. I used to like it. Now, I don't. "And you should see this dress I found. It's got a sexy, sheer bodice. You will love it."

"You've picked out a dress?" I ask incredulously. What. The. Ever. Loving. Fuck?

"Yes. I had all weekend to think about things. I called, but you didn't answer. Where were you? And who are you on the phone with?"

I look down and see that my phone is tightly pressed against my chest. "Oh, gosh. Ariela."

I examine my phone and see the call disconnected.

Shit.

Did she hang up on me? Did she hear what Shelby said? Does she hate me?

How can this be happening now?

"Ariela?" Shelby shrills. "Is she the girl who wouldn't have a threesome?" She rolls her eyes. "Obviously, *that* won't last long. You need someone like me, a lady on the red carpet and a freak in the bed. Speaking of that, when is the next premiere?"

"I, uh—"

"That's okay, baby. We'll worry about it later. We should talk about more pressing matters, like the wedding. I know they are hard to plan on short notice, but we should do it up right, don't you think? And I found the name of the wedding planner who did Blake Lancaster's wedding. They flew all their guests to Paris and had a whole week of parties. Wouldn't that be so amazing?"

I feel like I'm going to puke. "You can stop with the wedding talk, Shelby. We are *not* getting married."

"But—"

"No buts. I'll take responsibility for the baby if it's mine, and I will be part of its life—but that's it."

Shelby's lip puffs into a pout. She curls her shoulders to give me a clear shot of her cleavage as she gets teary. "You don't have any idea what it's like to grow up in a house without a father."

"No, I do not."

"I don't want that for our baby, Riley. I want it to have a home. And speaking of that, I think I should move in with you. My place is shitty, and I don't think Riley Johnson would want his baby growing up in such a place."

"I've never seen where you live. I really don't know anything about you. Do you have a job?" How is it possible that I got a girl pregnant who I know nothing about? Especially when the only girl I ever wanted to get pregnant is finally back in my life.

"Of course I have a job. I'm a cocktail waitress. That's how we met."

"No, we met when you sat down next to me at a bar."

"It wasn't very busy that night, so they let me off early. Melanie, who's a bitch, was bragging that she was waiting on you and Knox Daniels and how she was gonna get a big tip. I told her big deal, that I was going home with you. And I did. To Paris. It was the most amazing first date ever."

While she's rambling, I'm worrying about what Ariela may have heard. I've got to call her back.

"So, let's worry about the details later. I need to make a business call," I lie, "and need some privacy. I'll call you later this week after I've had some time to digest this."

And call my lawyer, I think to myself.

"Oh, that's okay. I won't bother you. I brought my stuff. It's all downstairs. While you make your call, I'll get myself settled."

"Shelby, you are *not* moving in with me."

No fucking way.

"If you saw my place, you wouldn't say that."

"Then I'll go see your place soon—after we have a paternity test."

"A paternity test? Seriously?"

"Yes, seriously."

"You're the only person I've slept with, I swear. I love you."

"Okay, time to go," I say, ushering her to the elevator. She's the last person I want to hear those three little words from.

"But I don't want to go," she pouts. Honestly, I'm a little shocked at her pouting.

"Shelby, I'm in shock over all this. Give me a few days to think about things, and I will get back to you." I expect her to drop to her knees, like she usually does when she doesn't get her way. In the past, she was very good at convincing me to do whatever she wanted when my dick was in her mouth. The fact that she doesn't worries me. That's how she managed to attend all three premieres rather than just the Paris one.

She starts bawling.

"I don't want to be pregnant and alone. We used condoms, Riley. I didn't *want* to get pregnant. It just happened. But now that I am, I'm so happy it's your baby. We'll have a beautiful life together. I've seen the pictures here of you with your family. Please don't abandon me. Please don't make me go through this alone."

I sigh. "I won't. I promise. And if your place is shitty, I'll find you somewhere beautiful to live."

Her eyes brighten, and she throws her arms around me. "Really?"

"Yes, just go home now, and we'll get things figured out this week."

Apparently, this has appeased her for the time being, because she allows me to escort her downstairs and send her home with all of her belongings.

I GO BACK up the elevator, sit myself down on the sofa, and bury my face in my hands.

Pregnant?

What a fucking nightmare.

I take my phone out of my pocket and stare at it, knowing I need to call Ariela back.

But I can't right now.

I don't know what the fuck to say.

So I text her with a lame excuse.

ASHER VINEYARDS - SONOMA COUNTY

Ariela

Riley: *Hey, I have some business to deal with here and I'll call you later.*

Business? I think.

How can leather-strap, threesome Shelby be classified as business?

SUNDAY, OCTOBER 12TH
DAWSON'S BEACH HOUSE – MALIBU
Vanessa

"IT'S TIME FOR bed," Dawson says to the girls, who are already dressed in pajamas and in their shared bedroom.

"Thanks for letting me go to the pumpkin patch with you today," I say, giving them each a hug.

"But I'm not tired!" Harlow insists, even though her eyes tell a different story.

"You have a big day tomorrow," Dawson says. "You need to get a good night's sleep."

"I'm excited to visit the school," Ava says, looking up from her phone.

"Who are you texting?" he asks.

"Everyone."

"Like who?"

"Mostly, I'm talking to Grandma and Fallon. Fallon is telling me all about the kids in her class. She likes a fifth grade boy named Keegan, but her friend likes him too. She says all the cute boys are in fifth grade."

"You're only in fourth grade, besides, I think you're

a little young to be worrying about that."

"Daddy." She audibly sighs and gives him a huge eye roll. "I've had boyfriends before."

He runs his hand roughly through his hair, looking stressed.

"Chill out, Dad," she says. "I won't get serious with a boy until at least middle school."

"More like college, if I have any say in it," he mutters.

"Miss Vanessa, will you tuck us in?" she asks, obviously wanting to end their boy conversation.

"Sure. I'd love to."

Dawson gives each girl a kiss, tells them goodnight, and then leaves.

I TUCK THEM into bed then read a story about a princess and a pony.

I'm ready to say goodnight when Harlow asks, "Do you want to marry my daddy?"

"Well, I'm not sure yet. You need to date and get to know someone before you get married."

"No," she disagrees, shaking her head. "Sometimes you meet a cute boy, and he saves you, and then after you kiss, you need to get married."

"That's how it works in princess stories and movies, but not in real life."

"But you told Daddy you love him, and when you are in love you are supposed to get married."

Ava lifts her head. "How come you cried when you told Daddy you love him?" She's been texting, and I didn't think she was listening.

"Do you know how babies are born?"

"I know!" Harlow raises her hand. "The baby grows in the mommy's tummy until it's big enough to be born."

Ava rolls her eyes. I have a feeling she knows more.

"And it starts out small, like a seed. It's itty bitty bitty," Harlow continues.

"I was pregnant once, but the baby died before it was born. The playroom was supposed to be for my baby when it got bigger."

Harlow launches herself at me, wrapping her little arms tightly around my waist.

"I'm sorry your baby died. Is it in Heaven with my mama? Maybe she can take care of your baby there, and you can take care of us here."

"Seems like your daddy does a pretty good job of taking care of you."

"He does," Ava says with a smile. "He can even braid my hair. I think talking about boys sort of freaks him out, though. He still thinks I'm a little girl."

"But since Daddy came here, Grandma has been taking care of us," Harlow interrupts. "We had to move in with Grandma after Mama died. I didn't want to leave our house, cuz I thought she might come back. But she didn't. Miss Vanessa, do you cry a lot?"

"Only when I'm sad."

"Mama was sad a lot."

"That's because she had depression," Ava says. "She had something wrong in her brain that made her feel sad even when she was happy."

"I think a pony would make *me* happy!" Harlow screams, pointing to her chest. "I want Daddy to buy me one, but he said he can't afford a pony."

"That's because Momma spent all Daddy's money.

At least that's what Grandma said," Ava whispers.

I try to hide my surprise at her comment and make a mental note to ask Dawson what she's talking about. How could she have spent all of his money?

"Ponies *are* expensive," I reply. "And not only do you have to buy one, you have to feed it and have a place for it to live."

"There's nowhere to keep a pony here on the beach, Harlow," Ava agrees.

Harlow's eyes get big, and she puffs out her lower lip, looking ready to cry. "But Miss Vanessa has a barn. My pony could live with her ponies. My pony could make pony friends. Just like we'll make new friends at our new school!"

Dawson pops into the doorway. "Miss Vanessa must be reading a really long story."

Harlow stands up, bouncing on the bed. "Yay, Daddy! Miss Vanessa says my pony can live at her house and make pony friends!"

I start to open my mouth to explain.

"I'm not buying you a pony right now, Harlow. We have to decide if we're even going to live here for sure. You have to see if you like the school first."

Dawson mentioning not staying is like a dagger to my heart. I realize that my happiness is resting on the girls' decision.

So, I decide to sweeten the pot.

I mean, a little old-fashioned bribery never hurt anyone. Right?

"Tell you what, Harlow. If you end up moving to California, I will let you adopt one of my ponies."

Her eyes get huge, and she hugs me. "Yay! I get a

pony! I get a pony!"

Dawson gives them each a hug, tucks them in again, says goodnight, and then leads me out of their room.

RILEY'S PENTHOUSE - L.A.

Riley

I WANT TO call Dallas and discuss this with him, but he and RiAnne just had their own baby, and the last thing he needs to deal with is more of my drama.

I could call my brother, but his girls are in town and might overhear our conversation.

So, I press Keatyn's number.

"Hey, Riley," she says, sounding out of breath.

"What are you doing?"

"Oh, Aiden and I were walking on the beach when I heard my phone ringing up on the deck, so I ran. What's up?"

"I know you just spent all weekend with me but, um, could I come over?"

"Sure, Marvel is making us a late dinner of that barbecued shrimp you love."

Although I'm in no mood to eat, I say, "Awesome. I'll be right over."

I CHANGE CLOTHES and head out.

The whole way there, I'm trying to process this all.

What it means for me.

What it means for me and Ariela.

I expect to ease the pregnancy into the conversation at some point during the evening, but the first thing out of my mouth when Keatyn opens the front door is, "Shelby's pregnant and wants to get married."

"What? Ohmigosh, Riley. You and Ariela just—"

"Yeah, I know," I say, hanging my head in defeat.

She wraps me in a hug, probably because she can tell I need one. "It will be okay, Riley. Go sit on the deck with Aiden. I'll get you a drink."

"You should probably bring the bottle," I mutter, even though I know she won't.

But she surprises me when she sets a twenty-five-year-old scotch on the table along with two glasses.

"What's wrong?" Aiden immediately asks.

"Shelby is pregnant and wants to get married," she tells him.

Aiden looks at me shrewdly. "And you believe her?"

"It's not like she's the first girl to tell me she's pregnant. I'm a little ashamed to admit this, but I keep a stash of pregnancy tests in the bathroom for such an occasion. She's the first girl to make the line turn pink. She's definitely pregnant."

"You've told me before that you always use condoms," Aiden says. "Did one fail?"

"Not that I was aware of but, obviously, one did since she's pregnant."

"Were you drunk when you were with her?"

"No, it was premiere week. All business."

Keatyn raises an eyebrow at me.

I roll my eyes. "Fine. It wasn't all business with Shelby, but I was never drunk when I was with her."

"What do you know about her?" Keatyn asks.

"Not much, other than her sexual preferences, and I'm well acquainted with her body but, beyond that, nothing personal. She suggested we get married right away. Has even found her dream dress."

"Riley, you aren't marrying her!" Keatyn gasps. "You can't!"

"And you need a paternity test," Aiden agrees.

"Do you have to wait until the baby is born for that?" I ask, taking a slug of scotch. I know I'm supposed to be sipping it, but fuck. I'd say this warrants it.

Marvel interrupts our conversation when he brings a charcuterie and cheese tray out for us along with a cucumber-infused water for Keatyn. "Dinner will be served shortly. Will Mr. Johnson be joining you?"

"Yes, he will be. Thank you, Marvel," Keatyn replies. Once he shuts the door, she scoops up a handful of almonds. "I would think you could test for paternity when they do the amniocentesis, but many women are against that because it's invasive."

"Invasive?" I ask, feeling dumb.

"In some cases, the test could harm the baby."

Aiden holds up his phone. "It says here there is new paternity testing technology that is noninvasive and can be done anytime after the eighth week."

"Riley, do you know anything about this girl?" Aiden asks again.

"I haven't been very picky about who I date," I admit.

"*Date* isn't really the right word for it," Keatyn mutters under her breath.

"I heard that, and you're right. Since Ariela and I broke up, I haven't *wanted* to know anything about them."

Tears form in Keatyn's eyes. I know she's pregnant and emotional, but I also know it's because she loves me. Especially when she reaches across and gives my arm a squeeze.

"The fact that she wants a quickie wedding concerns me," Aiden, ever the voice of reason, says.

"You're having a quickie wedding cuz you knocked up Keatyn," I tease.

Aiden gives me the eye and is ready to tear me a new one, but Keatyn grabs ahold of his hand and intervenes. "I can kind of sympathize with Shelby on that part," she says. "I've been in a long relationship with Aiden and when the line turned pink that was the first thing I thought of. How I'm not married. How I don't want to raise the baby alone. And once I got over the shock of it, I started worrying about bringing up the baby in the best environment and all that stuff."

Aiden starts to say something, but Keatyn holds her hand up and continues. "You both just need a little time to process it all."

"She said she grew up without a dad. I wanted to tell her I could care less, but if it is my baby—speaking of that, is it even possible? Like from a timing standpoint? I don't understand all that ovulation stuff Dallas is always going on about."

"That's because they use the rhythm method of birth control."

"What is that?"

"It's a contraceptive method where you decide

when to have sex based on a woman's cycle."

"They have five kids."

"And all but the first and last were planned. When was the first time you and Shelby were together?"

"The Paris premiere."

"Which was on September the twenty-third." She sets her phone down and counts out days on her calendar. "Twenty days ago. Which is about right, Riley. A woman's cycle is roughly twenty-eight days long. You typically ovulate in the middle of that, at around day fourteen. So, more than likely, she's about five weeks pregnant."

"Five weeks? How can that be? I've known her for less than three weeks."

"It's complicated," Aiden says. "But basically the two weeks of a woman's cycle *before* she gets pregnant count in how far along she is. They go by the first day of her last period rather than the conception date like you would assume."

"The timing works, Riley. She would have just missed her period, done the test, had it turn positive, and here you are."

"Now I feel bad for not believing her," I say, sliding further down in my chair.

Marvel comes outside, interrupting us again. "Dinner is served in the dining room."

"Would it be too much trouble for us to eat out here tonight?" Keatyn asks him sweetly. "It's such a beautiful evening."

"But of course," he says.

As soon as the door shuts, Aiden pours each of us more scotch. "Riley, how many people did you sleep with last month?"

"Uh."

"Exactly. She could have, too."

"Yeah, I guess, but she said she hasn't. She says she's in love with me."

"You're a big target, Riley," Keatyn says. "If she doesn't know who the father is, she might go with the one who could provide the most."

"That's why you have to do a paternity test," Aiden says. "*Have* to."

I sigh for about the hundredth time since I learned about the pregnancy. "Ariela and I were talking about kids on the phone tonight. I always thought maybe—"

"You would have kids with her?" Keatyn asks, finishing my sentence.

"Yeah."

"So, you already know that you want a relationship with her? I thought you were deciding at the wedding."

"Yeah. I mean, we're supposed to talk this week. Obviously, she needs to get a divorce. But, yes, I think I do want to be with her. I can't believe that she finally comes back into my life and this happens. I don't want a pregnancy to screw things up for us. But, if the baby is mine, I'll want to be with it, not just see it on weekends."

"Then you get custody, or at least joint custody," Aiden states. "You don't have to live with the mother to do so."

"I know. And I don't want to live with her. But she's a nice girl. I mean, what I know of her. When she was talking about getting married and moving in, I was thinking she was a gold digger, but then she talked sincerely about family. She also said she lives in a dive. I don't want the mother of my baby living in a dive."

"Then rent her an apartment if you need to, Riley, but nothing else until we get a paternity test," Aiden says.

Marvel comes back out with place settings, so I excuse myself. "I'm going to call and talk to her. I feel bad about the way I reacted."

I dial Shelby's number.

"Hey, it's Riley."

"I'm surprised to hear from you already," she says.

"Yeah, about that. Look, I'm sorry for my behavior earlier. Believe it or not, I've had a few girls tell me they are pregnant in an effort to—whatever. Anyway, I just want you to know that I'm going to find you a new place to live. Somewhere close to me, so I can take care of you while you're pregnant, and I can see the baby a lot once it's born."

"Aww, Riley," she cries. "That makes me so happy. I don't want my baby to grow up without a daddy."

"I don't want that either."

"It would be a lot easier if I just moved in with you," she suggests.

"No offense, but I really don't know much about you. I can't commit to something like that yet."

"You know everything you need to know, Riley. You know how to make me moan. That's all I need. I know you're loaded, and I'm sure you have to worry, but I'm not like that. I grew up with nothing, and it's what I'm used to. I don't need a big fancy place to live. But I do want our baby somewhere safe."

"I do too."

"You swear you won't abandon me?"

"I swear, Shelby."

"I was so worried. I'm not sure how I'm going to make this month's rent. I missed a bunch of shifts when I traveled with you, and I've been sick and throwing up all week."

"I'll take care of your rent. Don't worry about anything. Your job is to keep our baby healthy. We can do the paternity test in a month, once you are eight weeks pregnant. If it's mine, you won't have to worry about money ever again."

"Thank you," she sobs.

WHEN I SIT back down at the table, Aiden says, "We started without you. You know how Marvel is about eating when the food is at its perfect temperature."

I place a napkin across my lap and dig in, letting the shrimp melt in my mouth.

"I didn't mean to eavesdrop, Riley," Keatyn says, "but I couldn't help but overhear. I'm really proud of how you handled that."

"And I'm wary, but I agree with her. You're a good man. Speaking of that," Aiden says with a grin. "Would you stand up for me at the wedding? Be my best man?"

I laugh even though I'm touched. "Does that mean I get to throw you an epic Vegas bachelor party?"

Keatyn tilts her head and glares at me.

I hold up my hands. "Just kidding. How about a round of golf with the guys this week instead?"

"That sounds great. Speaking of great," he says after taking a sip of his drink, "before you got here, Keatyn was telling me about the offer to sell Captive."

"The more I think about it, the more I like the idea. Hell, maybe I'll buy a place in the country."

"Really?" Keatyn asks.

"Yeah, really. Dallas and RiAnne have their horse farm in Kentucky, and you and Aiden have this house, the vineyard, plus homes in Paris and New York."

"And London," Aiden coughs.

"London?" Keatyn and I both say at the same time.

He nods and says to Keatyn, "You'll be filming there. I don't want you in a hotel."

"We're also filming in Prague and Dubai. Did you buy places there, too?"

"No, I looked at your schedule. You'll only be in those two cities for a week apiece. Most of the time will be spent in Paris, New York, and London. Although, I don't know how much rest you'll get. Knox seems to think he's staying with you. And Marvel, of course, is going. Not to mention your security."

She leans over and gives him a kiss. "You're the sweetest boy ever," she says, making me want to call Ariela. How am I going to tell her about Shelby?

"Where do you want another house, Riley?" she asks.

"Well, if you and Knox are going to build a studio in the sticks, I would think I'd want to be close."

"Maggie offered Ariela a job at the vineyard," Aiden says.

"Doing what?"

"Originally, she offered her the role of fundraising coordinator to handle all our events around the world. But Logan and Grandpa think we should expand our event venue with some larger spaces, maybe a barn like

25

ours and a small onsite hotel to house guests. We thought she could oversee that. Create the perfect venue."

"Sounds expensive," I say.

Aiden points at Keatyn. "Not any more expensive than her building Captive North."

I chuckle. "I suppose you're right."

Keatyn looks at her phone and frowns. "Um, I just got a text from Maggie."

"What about?"

"She asked if I've talked to you tonight and, um—"

"What else?"

"She wants to know if you got a girl pregnant."

"Oh, shit," I say. "That means Ariela heard what Shelby said. And I haven't called her back. I texted her and said I had business. We're just getting started again. What am I supposed to say?"

"Tell her the truth, Riley," Keatyn says.

DAWSON'S BEACH HOUSE – MALIBU

"ADOPT A PONY, huh?" I tease Vanessa. "You must really want me to stay."

"Stop with the cocky grin."

"You like me."

She laughs and then sits on my lap. "I do like you."

"Sweetening the deal with a pony was brilliant. But what I want to know is what *I* get if I move here permanently?"

She lowers her head and places her delicious lips on mine. "Me."

I'm ready to throw her on the couch and show her what else she'll get when a little voice says, "Daddy?"

Vanessa quickly moves off my lap.

"What do you need, Harlow?" I ask, getting up and scooping her into my arms.

"A hug," she says. "I can't sleep. What if the kids at school don't like me?"

"They will love you. How could they not? You are smart and funny."

"Carder told me he thinks I'm pretty. Do you think I'm pretty?"

"I think you are beautiful, both inside and out."

"You can't see inside me, silly Daddy."

"That means inside, you have a good heart. A kind soul."

"Like, I'm nice?"

"Yes. Have you ever met someone who is pretty on the outside, but who isn't very nice to people?"

"Like the evil stepmother in the princess movie?"

"Exactly like that."

"Carder said he would be my friend. That he would sit by me if the teacher would let him."

"See, so you will already have a friend if you like the school."

"Ava asked Grandma what happens if we hate it. And she isn't sure about leaving her best friend."

"If you hate it when we visit, you have to tell me. There are other schools we can look at."

"I miss you, Daddy," she says with a yawn, and

puts her head on my shoulder.

I gently sway with her for a few minutes and say a prayer that tomorrow will go well. I need my girls with me.

I glance over at Vanessa, who is watching me intently. I nod my head in the direction of the girls' bedroom and carry Harlow back to bed, tucking her in and kissing her forehead.

I SIT BACK down next to Vanessa.

"You're such a good dad," she says, her eyes glistening. I wish I could take away her pain.

"I hope this is the right thing for them."

"Being with you is the right thing," she says, pulling me into my bedroom and locking the door behind us.

She pushes me onto the bed, causing me to land with a thud on my back. I lean up to grab her, but she puts a high heel square on my chest, holding me in place.

I glide my hand up her leg. "That's a little dangerous. You might stab me."

She presses just a teeny bit harder, her heel digging in a little, but she doesn't say a word.

She doesn't really need to, since she's unbuttoning her blouse.

"I'd like to lean up and kiss that sexy shoulder, but I'm afraid you might injure me." I caress her foot as she sheds her blouse. "These might be the hottest shoes I've ever seen."

"You haven't seen anything yet," she challenges.

A challenge I will happily accept.

ASHER VINEYARDS – SONOMA COUNTY
Ariela

AFTER PACING IN my room for twenty minutes, I decide I need some wine and someone to talk to, so I go over to Maggie's house.

Logan asks me a barrage of questions about Eastbrooke's homecoming, which I politely answer. But the nagging in my head gets so strong I just blurt out, "I think Riley got a girl pregnant."

"Why do you think that?" Maggie asks.

I give them a replay of our phone conversation and what I think I heard.

"And then he texted you and said he had *business*?" Maggie asks incredulously.

"Honestly, I'm surprised Riley doesn't already have kids," Logan says. "He definitely gets around."

"Logan!" Maggie says, giving him the evil eye.

"It's okay," I say. "I know why he's been doing what he's been doing, and I understand it. Plus, I can't say much since I'm married."

"Regardless, I want to know what's going on," Maggie says. "I'm texting Keatyn."

"Do you think she will know?"

Maggie squints her eyes at me. "You know how tight they were in high school. Times that by more than ten years."

I watch as she sends out a text, and I stare at her expectantly.

"There are little dots, like she's typing something, but then they disappear. That usually means she doesn't know what to say."

My phone vibrates on the table. "Oh, shit," Logan says. "It's Riley. Ten bucks says he's with Keatyn and Aiden. You better answer that."

"Yeah, I guess I should." I hit the button and say, "Hey, Riley."

"Yeah, so sorry about our call. Um, it's been kind of a crazy night."

Part of me wants to immediately ask if what I heard is what she said, but the other part of me—probably the part who has a husband she doesn't trust—wants to test him. To see what he will tell me on his own.

He continues. "I had some personal business to take care of. I'm not sure what you heard before the call disconnected."

Personal business. I sigh with relief.

"Are you still there?" he asks, his voice soft but stressed. I want to reach my hand through the phone and caress his face.

"It's okay, Riley," I say instead.

"I don't know if you will say that once I tell you this, but Shelby—"

"The girl who was in your place that night?"

"Yes. She's pregnant."

"Did you date long?"

"No. We had a total of three dates—the three movie premieres—and used a condom every time. There was never any evidence of failure, but she's pregnant. I made her do a pregnancy test and everything."

"Are you sure it's yours?" I ask gently.

"Keatyn tells me the timing's right. But we'll be doing a paternity test as soon as possible. If it is mine, I have to be a good father, Ariela."

"I wouldn't expect you to be anything else."

"Can you—can we—if we decide to go forward—handle this? God, Ariela, you are the only one I ever wanted to have a baby with. When I heard you didn't have any children, I took it as another sign. That you were waiting for us to get back together. That we were meant to be. That maybe it was fate."

"And what do you think now, Riley?"

"I think fate is a tricky bitch."

I laugh. "Brooklyn said that to Keatyn in the movie."

I laugh too. "Yeah, he did. He used to say it a lot. God, I miss him."

"You were all close?"

"He was one of my best friends. After it happened, I almost—I got on the plane and everything . . ."

"Almost what?"

"Came to find you. We were all devastated. And Aiden said something about never wasting a moment of our lives. I got on my plane and flew to Connecticut, but I had chickened out by the time I got there. I was afraid you would say you never wanted to see me again or that you were married or something, and I knew my heart couldn't take it."

"Oh, Riley," I say, tears filling my eyes. "You have no idea how much that touches me. That you thought of me in that moment."

"Does that mean you're not mad about Shelby?"

"It happened before I came to California, Riley. I can't be mad about it." It's the right thing to say, but I'm not sure if I mean it. I am mad about it. And the event planner in me is ticking off all the ways this could go wrong. All the hurdles and obstacles that could get in the way if we decide to have a relationship. Our love would be tested in ways we never expected. I hear a muffled noise. "Riley, are you okay?"

"Yeah, sorry," he says. "It's like I've been holding my breath since she said *I'm pregnant*. I was worried you might think I'm not worth the hassle."

"Riley, I'm still married. If we go forward, it isn't going to be easy. And to quote another line from Brooklyn, *Life is messy. It's supposed to be that way.*"

He lets out a frustrated sigh. "I don't want it to be. We're supposed to talk about us this week. Get to know each other again. Do you still want that?"

"Yes, I do. And, Riley, we don't really have to decide at the wedding if we want to date. We can take our time. Get to be friends again first."

"I'm tired," he says.

"I am too. Let's say goodnight."

"Like we used to?" I can hear the boy in his voice.

"Just like we used to. Go."

"I'll be dreaming of you," we say in unison.

SHELBY'S APARTMENT - THE VALLEY

As I ENTER my crappy apartment, I run my hand across my belly and think about how Riley took the news. Honestly, I thought an honest man like him would let me move in right away.

I slam the door shut hard, pissed that I'm back here and not sitting pretty in Riley's penthouse, planning our wedding. The things a girl has to do to get ahead in this city.

My roommate yells at me, "Well, how'd it go?"

"Come out here and talk to me. I need a drink."

"You shouldn't be drinking when you're pregnant," she says, coming out of her bedroom and plopping down on our second-hand sofa. I study the golden color of the velvet fabric—make that third or fourth hand.

"I drank before I knew I was pregnant. I don't think one more will hurt."

"That baby is your golden ticket out of here. You should take good care of it."

"True," I say, grabbing a glass out of the dishwasher. "Are these clean?"

She shrugs. "Maybe."

I hold the glass up to the light. "There's lipstick on the corner. I'll just rinse it out." I run the wine glass—one of the two we own—under hot water, then cold, then fill it to the rim from a box of white zinfandel in the refrigerator. "You want one?"

"Please," she says, handing me her empty plastic cup, which is emblazoned with the logo of the sports bar she works days at.

"So, how did he take the news?" she asks as we make ourselves comfortable on the couch.

"He was shocked. I mean, that's to be expected, right?"

"Right."

"Then he was kind of an ass. That did surprise me. He actually made me take a pregnancy test right then and there."

"Well, thank God you're really pregnant."

"Can you imagine? He keeps pregnancy tests like all the time because girls say they are preggers when they aren't to try and trap him."

"That's pretty tacky, if you ask me," she says. "But he is rich. I'm sure he has to worry about gold diggers."

We share a knowing glance and then both start giggling.

"Was he ever surprised when the test turned positive right away. I even pretended to be worried about it. Told him it might not turn pink since it was so early."

"That was a nice touch. What did he say when you suggested moving in?"

"He said it was too fast. Of course, then I suggested we get married right away. I think that spooked him a little, plus he was talking on the phone when I got there. Remember the night I got his doorman to let me in and was waiting for him in that little strappy costume?"

"Oh, yeah. He showed up with some other chick, right?"

"Yeah. When he came in the building, he was

talking to her on the phone—sounding all lovey-dovey."

"So she could be a problem?"

"Maybe, but I have a bigger problem."

"What's that?"

"He wants a paternity test."

She takes a big sip of her wine, sloshing a little onto the couch—obviously it's not her first cup of the night. "That gives you seven months to get him to marry you."

"Wrong. I have *one* month. Apparently, they can test after eight weeks. Did you know they could do it so soon?"

"No. I thought they couldn't tell until after the baby was born."

"That's what I thought too."

"You're already eight weeks!"

"Yeah, but he doesn't know that."

"Then you better work fast, girl."

"Oh, I plan to."

"And what about the baby's real father?"

"Larry? He's a bartender. I didn't come to California to starve. But the good news is Riley said he'd find me a place to live, and he'd take care of me."

"Then what?"

"We sleep together, of course. A lot. He likes it naughty, and I can do naughty. I'll have him down on his knees begging for more."

"More like you'll be down on your knees," she quips.

"Ha. True. He does like that. Of course, what guy doesn't? Anyway, that preppy little bitch who looked horrified when I suggested a threesome is no match for me."

"Game on," my friend says.

"I'll drink to that," I agree, clinking my glass against hers. "You would have been proud of me. I gave the performance of my life. Cried when appropriate. Was offended when I needed to be. I still don't understand why I've never gotten an acting job."

"You manage to land Riley and keep your body after the baby, and you won't ever need to work again."

"True," I say, dreamily imagining the rest of my life as one glitzy diamond-and-designer filled movie premiere.

MONDAY, OCTOBER 13TH
KEATYN & AIDEN'S HOME – MALIBU
Keatyn

"ARE YOU SURE I shouldn't go to the doctor with you?" Aiden asks as his lips graze across my shoulder.

"I'm sure. It's just a check-up, besides, you need to be at the vineyard today to give that foundation a tour. It will be a big deal if Moon Wish teams up with them."

"I know, but I'm wondering if it's too big. We've always tried to help smaller causes where the funds really make a difference."

"But the publicity from teaming up with them will put Moon Wish on the map with major philanthropists, not just people who follow celebrities. And that, in turn, will help us reach more people in the long run so that we can continue to make a difference with the smaller causes."

He pulls me in tighter. "You're right. Overall it's a good thing, but it's going to require a lot of travel on my part if it all goes through."

"As long as your trips don't interfere with our honeymoon and end by the time I'm done filming, it will be fine. We're used to crazy schedules."

"Not for much longer," he says, caressing my belly. "Can you believe that in less than a week you will finally be Mrs. Aiden Arrington?"

I sigh happily. "I love that name. In fact, I love it so much, I'm keeping it."

"You won't have much choice after we're married," he says with a laugh.

"I mean professionally, Aiden. I'm going to be Keatyn Arrington."

"Really? Are you sure that's a good career move?"

"Ha! You sound like Vanessa."

"You don't have to do that for me," he says, his hand burning a trail down my side and leaving me breathless.

"I'm not doing it for you." I roll on top of him and kiss his neck. "I'm doing it for me."

AFTER A SEXY send-off, I'm at the doctor's office.

"So how are you feeling?" my obstetrician asks me.

"Pretty good, overall. A little morning sickness. Strong smells seem to bother me—or maybe it's that things smell stronger than usual."

"Are you taking it easy? Getting enough rest? Eating well?"

"I'm definitely sleeping more than normal, and I'm pretty worn out by the end of the day. Whenever we get a break in filming, I always used to work, but instead I've been napping. And, I've probably been eating a little too well," I say, patting my stomach, which seems to have popped out over the last few days.

"That's good to hear. How's your work schedule going to be during your pregnancy?"

"We wrap up filming here on Thursday, then I'm off for three weeks. After that, I'll be filming on locations around the world. We'll be gone for about three months and then I'll be off until the baby is born."

"Very good. We're going to do an ultrasound today. I'd like to see what's going on in there."

"But we don't have an ultrasound scheduled. Is something wrong?"

"Your blood test shows that your hCG levels are a little higher than I would expect at this stage of the game."

"That's the pregnancy hormone? Is high bad?"

"It's not bad, but we need to take a look so we can determine your actual due date. Your levels suggest you could be further along."

"But I had my period last month. How could I be—"

"Let's just take a look."

"But Aiden should be here. We wanted to do the ultrasound together. See our baby for the first time together!"

"We'll be checking for a heartbeat and taking some measurements today. Would you like to call and have him come in?"

I shake my head. "I can't. He flew up to the vineyard for the day, and I won't have time to come back this week. I guess we should do it now."

While they get the ultrasound started, I try not to

panic.

But it's hard not to.

Why aren't my hormone levels normal? What does that mean? What if something is wrong with our baby?

I glance over at the screen even though I don't want to. It's like watching a horror movie with my hands over my face, peeking through my fingers.

The doctor and ultrasound tech are studying the screen intently. And the concern on both their faces is evident. I also haven't heard a heartbeat. What if there isn't one? What will I do if he tells me something is wrong? How would I tell Aiden?

I look closer and try to figure out what they are seeing. All I see is what looks like static, but then the movement stops, and they focus on a dark circle.

The tech nudges the doctor.

"Is there something wrong?" I ask.

"Do you see that, there?" The doctor points to the screen as it flickers, showing us the dark circle from a different angle. One that allows me to see there's something inside it.

"Ohmigosh, is that the baby? Is it okay?"

"It is okay," the doctor says. "Do you see that flicker? That's the baby's heart beating."

"It's beautiful."

"And don't worry. I expect your pregnancy to continue normally," he tells me. "This will just cause a few wrinkles."

"A few—" I start to ask.

The tech, who has been clicking away, interrupts me. "Eight weeks and two days for this one."

"This *one?*"

"Yes," the doctor says with a grin. "Show her."

The tech zooms out, and I can see that there are two little dark circles with two little flickers inside.

"Twins," the doctor says.

"Twins?" I repeat in shock. "Is that why I'm starting to show so early?"

"Yes. And it's why your hormone levels are higher than normal. I suspected twins, since multiples run in your family, but wanted to be sure. Aiden will be pretty excited by this news, don't you think?"

"Yeah, he will be." I shake my head and look down at my the side of my hand, remembering when Inga read my palm in St. Croix years ago and predicted how many children I would have.

"Um, hang on," the tech says. "Look at this."

"Zoom back out," the doctor instructs. "Well, will you look at that sight. Something doctors don't see very often. Triplets."

"Triplets?"

"Yes, your mother was one of only two naturally conceived sets of triplets I've had the pleasure of delivering. You will be number three. Congratulations. I'm glad you have some scheduled time off toward the end of your pregnancy. You're going to need it."

When the ultrasound is over, he hands me a photo and sends me on my way.

When I get inside the town car waiting to take me to the studio, I burst into happy tears as I think about how I'm going to tell Aiden the news.

And when.

VANESSA'S ESTATE – HOLMBY HILLS

Vanessa

PEYTON IS AT my house. I discreetly texted her on Sunday and told her I wanted to redecorate and asked if she was free today.

"So, I want to get rid of everything and start over. Can we do it fast?"

Peyton is surveying the family room. "Do you really want to get rid of *everything*?"

I nod. "Yes."

"But look at the lines on this." She runs her hand across the back of a chair. "And this chair is leather. The fabric will stand up to kids and can be dressed down. You have so many amazing things to work with. I'll take an inventory of all the furniture, move it out to the garage, and we'll start over, bringing in pieces where they will work."

"I guess that's okay, if you can use some of it in a casual way. I just want it to be comfortable."

"Do you want *any* formal rooms? What about your dining room, living room, and the ballroom?"

"I can tell you that the only time I used those rooms were when Bam's family came to town. I'm pretty sure his mother sleeps fully dressed and made up." Peyton laughs. "You have kids. Make this house a place where they'd feel comfortable."

"I still think you need a few spaces that are more formal. For when you entertain, like during the holidays."

"That's a good point. So a few sort-of formal spaces."

Peyton studies me. "Are you doing all this for Dawson?"

"No, actually, I'm doing it for myself. I need a fresh start. Dawson and his girls were just the catalyst that made me realize it."

She gives me a smirk. "I like how you're dressed today." I look down at my cutoffs and bare feet. "I haven't seen you in something like that since I met you on the beach. And I think that was the only time."

"These are probably the same shorts," I laugh. "I need to find myself in this house, if that makes sense."

"It does," she says, scribbling something into the margin of the list she's making.

"Can I ask you a personal question?" I inquire.

"Sure," she says.

"If you and Damian divorced and you had never had children of your own—if you couldn't have children—would you adopt or would you assume that if you couldn't have them you weren't meant to?"

"I would adopt. Even if I were single. I wouldn't let my circumstances get in the way of my desire to be a mother."

"I need to show you one of the rooms that I don't want redone." I grab her hand, take her upstairs, and show her the playroom. "I'd like this room to stay the way it is."

"This room looks nothing like the rest of the house," she says, studying the decor.

"Maybe that's why I like it."

"Are you thinking about adopting, Vanessa?"

I nod. Now that I've told Dawson about not being able to have children, I'm able to tell her, too. "After my miscarriage, the doctor told me that I couldn't have children."

Peyton gives me a hug, her large baby bump crashing into me. "Oh, Vanessa, why didn't you tell us? That's such a devastating blow on top of losing your baby."

"Yeah, it was. It wasn't just Bam's infidelity that sent me on my downward spiral."

"I'm glad you're back at the top."

"Me too."

"You seem really happy."

"I am. You and Dawson's wife, Whitney, were close, right?"

"Yeah, she was my best friend for most of high school. I saw in *The Keatyn Chronicles* movies how Keatyn sort of revolted against you. I did the same thing to Whitney. But, really, I was revolting against myself."

"I saw the movie. Um, did you stay in touch with her after all that? I get the feeling there's something surrounding her death that Dawson isn't telling me."

"I went to her funeral even though we didn't stay friends. I felt bad for Dawson and his girls. All I really know is that she sent the girls to stay at his parents' house the night she did it, and Dawson was the one to find her. But, other than the fact she took her own life, I don't really know any other details. I'm still good friends with his older brother, Camden. He hated her, but after she died, he hated her more for what she did to Dawson."

"Right, but what did she do to him?"

"Isn't killing herself and leaving him with two small children to care for on his own enough?"

"Yes, of course, but there's more to the story. Last night, Ava said their mom spent all of their dad's money and that's why they moved in with their grandma."

"Now that you mention it, I did think it a little odd that Dawson moved in with his parents right after it happened. You'd think for the girls' stability he would have wanted them to stay in their home. But I assumed he moved because he needed the emotional support of his family."

"But if he didn't have money, why didn't he work for two years?"

"I know he quit to take care of the girls, but I assumed it was because he had the money to do so."

"Keatyn knows the whole story, but she won't tell me. She says it's his story to tell."

"Well, then, you should ask him," Peyton says, moving out of the playroom and peeking into each bedroom as we talk. "When we redo the bedrooms, would you like something more suited to younger guests?"

"Yes, and Ava is almost a teenager, so let's do this room in something she would think is way cool. And Harlow loves horses, so maybe something equestrian but still girly?"

"Got it. How soon do you want this all done?"

I raise an eyebrow at her.

She laughs. "Yesterday, right?"

"Yeah. Pretty much."

"Why don't you get out of my hair, while I go spend some time in each room and think about what I want to do. Tomorrow, I'll do some shopping and have workers empty everything out, so we can start with a clean slate. We'll move everything out to the garages, and I'll bring some pieces back in to use in different ways. It's going to be a bit of a disaster for a few days. Can you handle that?"

"I can."

"Seriously, Vanessa, is there anything in this house that you love?"

I sigh. "I love my closet a lot, and I think all the oriental rugs are beautiful, particularly the golden one in the area off the billiards room."

"What do you like about your closet?"

"It's the one room that I decorated only to my tastes."

She squints her eyes and says, "Then that's where I need to start."

CAPTIVE FILMS – SANTA MONICA

I GOT UP early this morning, finally giving up on trying to get a restful night's sleep. Even though Ariela seemed to take the news well, I could hear the stress in her voice.

As Tyler brings me coffee and a pastry, I absent-mindedly pat my midsection, feeling guilty for skipping my usual morning workout with my trainer.

"Raul said you bailed on him today. You feeling okay, boss?" Raul is Tyler's life partner and my personal trainer. "Still recovering from the big homecoming weekend?"

"I guess so," I say, not wanting to talk about it. "What do we need to discuss before I start my day?"

He studies me for a beat before looking down at the iPad he uses to keep track of everything. "Well, I took the liberty of ordering a gift for Dallas and RiAnne's baby. It will be delivered tomorrow morning."

"What did I get them?"

"A lovely Armani layette for the darling baby Farryn, a gorgeous Hermes bag for the new mother, and a golf outing with the new father."

"Are you talking about me?" Dallas asks from my doorway.

"What are you doing here? Shouldn't you be at home?" I ask him.

"RiAnne is going to be in the hospital for a couple days. I took the rugrats to school and both the nanny and RiAnne's mother are home with the little ones. I want to get the negotiations on the Captive deal done before Keatyn goes on her honeymoon."

"Wow, that's fast."

"They want to move fast, and I was under the assumption that you were on board."

"I am."

"Then we need to come up with a new name if we're going to give up Captive."

"Like what?"

"I was thinking something to do with the three of

us. Like Triad Films, maybe. Other synonyms for three are Trinity, Trio, Triplicity. Trivium. I actually like that one."

"Three, huh? Maybe we should go with Menage A Trois?" I joke. But then I think about Ariela's face when Shelby suggested a threesome. "Um, I need to talk to both of you about something. Tyler, will you close the door and have a seat?"

He does as I ask and then both he and Dallas sit in the chairs in front of my desk, looking at me expectantly.

"There is a new development in my life that I need you both to be aware of."

Dallas looks at me shrewdly. "You find out you have a kid?"

"Sort of. Shelby is pregnant."

"Do I know her?" Dallas asks.

"She was my date for the L.A. premiere."

"Cheap champagne girl?"

I nod. "Yes."

Dallas leans back, his hands forming a bridge as he thinks. "And you believe you're the father?"

"Part of me doesn't know how it's possible, since I used condoms, but the timing is right, and she is definitely pregnant. Aiden says there's a paternity test that can be done at eight weeks. She's about four weeks along."

"So, we wait until a paternity test determines you are the father then, once we know, we'll deal with the outcome."

"I told her I would find her somewhere nice to live."

"Why did you do that?" Tyler asks.

"Because I'm a nice guy, and if she is having my baby, I'm not going to be some asshole baby daddy. She lives in a shitty place, and I don't want the possible mother of my child living somewhere like that. She is also short on her rent this month because she's been sick."

"She's already asking you for money. That's a red flag, Riley," Dallas states.

"She wanted to move in with me."

"Oh dear," Tyler says.

"And suggested we get married," I confess.

"Gold digger," Tyler coughs.

"That was my first thought, as well," Dallas says.

"It was my first thought, too, but she told me she grew up with nothing and doesn't expect anything from me other than for me to be a good father. Apparently, her father wasn't around growing up."

"Well, that explains a few things," Dallas says with a chuckle. "Okay, serious advice from both your friend and your lawyer. Tyler, find her a place to live. I'll draw up a document for her to sign *before* she's allowed to move in that will spell out what happens if a paternity test doesn't prove you are the father. If that happens, we'll give her thirty days to vacate the premises. We'll deal with anything else once the results come back."

"That sounds good," I agree. "Tyler, find her a place that is furnished somewhere close to me but not too close. And I'd like it right away. Somewhere nice."

"I'm on it, Boss," he says. "Do you have anything else pressing for me this morning?"

"Take care of this first. Everything else can wait."

Tyler heads out, and Dallas goes over to the bar, grabs a bottle, and pours a shot in both our coffees. "How are you doing?"

"I'm in shock. I can't believe something like this would happen just when Ariela is finally back in my life."

"Did you tell her?"

"Yeah. She said it didn't matter. That she would love any baby of mine. I want to have children with Ariela, not Shelby."

"How's her divorce coming?"

"I'm not sure. It's not something we've talked about. Mostly because we weren't talking after the Vegas fiasco. Then at Eastbrooke, it wasn't the right place. Since she'll be working at the vineyard all week and I'll be here, we promised each other we'd have nightly phone conversations to get to know each other better. I'm sure the divorce subject will come up."

Knox strolls in with Jennifer, not bothering to knock. "Heard you knocked up the blow job chick."

"That is not for public knowledge," I say. "Tyler, get in here!"

Tyler comes rushing in. "What?"

"You are not to tell anyone about this until we get a paternity test."

"I haven't told anyone."

Jennifer sets a newspaper down in front of me. A headline is circled in red. *Captive Films' Riley Johnson's Baby Mama Drama.*

"Are you fucking kidding me?" I yell.

"The article got a lot of other stuff right," Jennifer says as I start reading.

Captive Films' Riley Johnson's Baby Mama Drama

Well, people. The goings-on at Captive Films just continue to get more exciting. We've learned that the playboy CEO, fresh back from his crazy Vegas publicity stunt with Knox Daniels, Jennifer Edwards, and his equally sexy brother, Dawson, is going to be a father.

The baby mama is a cocktail waitress at one of the establishments Riley frequents. Our source tells us that RBM (Riley's Baby Mama) was his date for all three of the world-wide premieres for The Keatyn Chronicles *trilogy. Although it's doubtful RBM will be hearing wedding bells soon with this notorious bachelor, the sounds of a wailing child should keep her occupied.*

Speaking of babies, Captive Films' CLO Dallas MacMahon welcomed a new addition to his family just yesterday. Mama and Baby number FIVE are said to be doing well.

Excitement surrounds this group. We're told by a source at the hospital that Dallas was out of town partying with Keatyn, Knox, and Riley when his wife went into labor. After a call that involved a whole lot of yelling, the friends flew home as fast as they could and were helicoptered to the hospital just in time for the birth.

All I know is this. I am not stepping foot in Captive Films. That pregnancy thing might just be catching.

Which brings me to my next revelation.

Hold on to your skirts, ladies. This is big

news.

I believe I may have been wrong. (I know, right? That never happens.)

But my being wrong leads to a whole lot of right.

Because this is juicy.

I have come to the conclusion that Keatyn's recent breast enhancement may NOT have been the result of plastic surgery.

I'm going on record. I'm going to be the first to call it.

Keatyn Douglas is pregnant.

Upon further inspection of all the photos from the recent Daddy's Angel *event, where Keatyn clung to Knox Daniels all night in a beautiful, tight Herve Leger bandage dress, I realized that I was too focused on her boobs to notice her small baby bump. Check out this side shot. Do you see what I see?*

Let the baby bump frenzy begin!

Now the question becomes—what kind of baby daddy drama will Keatyn have? Is the father of her child her fiancé, vintner Aiden Arrington, or is it Knox Daniels, her sexy costar, with whom her tangled relationship has burned bright for years?

Can you even imagine how beautiful a Knox—Keatyn spawn would be?

With Knox and Keatyn set to be on location together over the next few months, I predict that the two will work out their issues, that Keatyn will break her engagement, and Knox and Jen-

nifer Edwards' fledgling relationship will fail.

Then the question will become—when will Knox and Keatyn get married?

And can I pretty please get an invitation?

P.S. I take back my earlier statement. I'd totally brave the halls of Captive Films if it meant I could get knocked up by Knox freaking Daniels or one of the Johnson brothers.

After reading it, I look at Jennifer. "What else did the article get right, besides the part about Dallas?"

"Knox dumped me."

"Sugar," Knox says, tilting his head at her.

She flips him off.

Then smiles at him.

"We made a mutual decision to be friends since we are going to be working together," Knox says, sounding like he's reading from an official press release.

Jennifer rolls her eyes. "So what do you guys think? Is Keatyn just bloated? I mean, we all have our days. It's called being a woman. Or do you think she might really be pregnant?"

We all give her the same blank look, which makes us appear totally guilty.

"No shit? Wait a second. That fundraiser we got invited to. Are she and Aiden getting married?!" she screeches.

"Shh!" Knox covers her mouth with his hand just as Vanessa and my brother burst through the door.

"The more the merrier," I say sarcastically.

"Did you see this?" Vanessa asks, tossing the paper on my desk. "Is it true? Did you knock up the skank?"

"I'm not sure she qualifies as a skank," I defend.

"She offered to have a threesome with Ariela ten seconds after she met her. What would you call her?"

"Adventurous?" Dallas offers, causing everyone else to laugh. But then he continues. "Vanessa, why don't you and I go to my office and discuss the situation since there are numerous legal issues involved."

"Fine," she says with a huff, then points at me. "Don't think you're off the hook for not telling me about this."

"I just found out last night myself!"

"Whatever," she says, marching off.

"Looks like it's been a busy morning here," Dawson says, sitting on the sofa after pouring himself coffee.

"Where have you been?"

"The girls have their school visit today. I told you I'd be late."

"Shit, I forgot."

"Sounds like you have a lot going on. I'm just praying no one calls in tears begging to leave. What can I say? I kinda like it here."

"You and Vanessa are getting down and dirty," Knox says. "I like it. Alright, people. I'm off. Got a call time in twenty."

"Jennifer, you have a wardrobe fitting today, don't you?" Tyler asks. "If you'd like, I'll escort you down."

"As long as you escort me by some donuts and get me a cup of your amazing coffee on the way," she says, taking his arm and letting him lead her out of the room while Tyler beams.

Dawson moves from the couch to a chair in front of my desk.

54

"How are you doing?" he asks sincerely. "I remember how shocked I was when Whitney told me she was pregnant. At first, I didn't believe her."

"I didn't believe Shelby either. But I watched her pee on a stick. Watched the line turn pink. She's definitely pregnant. Just don't know for sure if it's mine, but I'm pretty sure that it is."

"Well, then, congrats, bro. Having children is a wondrous thing."

"I'm getting Shelby an apartment. Do you think that's stupid of me, not knowing for sure?"

"No, I don't. If she is the mother of your child, you want to treat her with respect, Riley."

"And if she's not?"

"Then you say goodbye and wish her the best."

I smile. "Thanks. I needed to hear that."

ASHER VINEYARDS – SONOMA COUNTY
Ariela

I'M OUTSIDE CHECKING the progress on the brick path Keatyn wanted installed when I notice a black town car pull up to the house.

Kyle gets out of the car and waves, so I go down to greet him.

"Asher Vineyards, huh? This looks like a pretty swanky place," he says, giving me a kiss on the cheek. "So is this really the land Keatyn gave to Aiden at the end of the movie?"

"Yes, they actually filmed that scene here."

"Can I see the spot where they stood?"

"Sure, come on. We can drop your bags off in one of the guest houses on the way."

"There's more than one guest house?"

"There are four on this property here. You'll be staying in one with me."

He gives me a devilish grin. "Are we sharing a bed?"

"No."

"Oh, I get it. You'll pretend you're sleep walking and accidentally fall on my dick."

I laugh. "I don't think so. But the other guest houses are being prepped for the family and friends who will be staying on site."

As we walk toward one of the little casitas, he says, "This looks like a normal house. I thought guest houses were supposed to be small."

"These aren't. Each one is about fifteen hundred square feet and feature two bedroom suites along with a small kitchen, living, and dining room. The one across the way there is larger and has three bedrooms." We drop his bags off and then continue to the spot.

"Is that an altar? I thought the party was a fundraiser."

"It is," I say carefully. "But there's going to be a wedding at it."

"Keatyn and Aiden got engaged recently," he says.

"Yes, they did. But the wedding is a vow renewal for Maggie and Logan."

"Logan was Aiden's best friend, played lacrosse, and was the Bad Prince in the school play, right?" he asks, citing what he knows from the movie.

"Yes, he and Maggie—"

"Dance team. Funny as shit. She and Logan got back together on the play stage," he interrupts.

I narrow my eyes at him.

He rolls his. "Fine. I went and saw the movie again and took notes. I figured I'd need to know who all the players are. So Logan and Maggie are married and they want to renew their vows and you have to plan not only a fundraiser but a wedding, too?"

"Exactly."

"Sweet. So what do you want me to do?"

I hand him a notebook filled with lists. "Start at the top and work your way down. Make sure everything is getting done. If it's not, come find me."

He leans in close to me. "Oh, don't worry, tonight, I'll come find you. Especially now that I know where you're sleeping."

"I lock my door," I tease.

"Won't matter. You'll be coming to me."

VANESSA'S ESTATE – HOLMBY HILLS

I'M JUST PULLING into my driveway when I get an unexpected call from Bam's mother.

"Vanessa, darling. How good it is to hear your voice."

"Thank you. Are you and Mr. Martinez well?"

"That is why I'm phoning you. My beloved husband is on death's doorstep."

"Oh, I'm so sorry. When did he become ill?"

"The doctors found cancer just a few months ago. It is aggressive and too advanced to do much other than keep him comfortable until he passes."

"Is there anything I can do for you?"

"Actually, there is. You and Juan must reconcile immediately."

"He's dating some model."

"They broke up."

"They did have quite an age difference," I say, trying my best to keep the snark out of my voice.

As in she was barely eighteen when he met her.

"You are a fine woman, Vanessa. Although, I didn't understand your need to work, I still respected it. But I think it's time that you and Juan settle down. Have a family."

"That will be kind of difficult since we got divorced," I reply flatly.

"I hear your tone, Vanessa. I know it well. I am not just an old woman pining for grandchildren. My son has changed his ways, as well. Please get in touch with him."

"With all due respect, Bam didn't love me enough not to cheat on me. And you barely tolerated my existence."

"Yes, well, it is difficult for any woman to compete with the love a mother has for her son. In retrospect, I may have been a little hard on you. For that I apologize."

"Thank you."

"Perfect. Now you will get back together and have

children. It is time."

The way she says it is very commanding, like she can just wish it, and it will happen.

"When we lost our child, your son was in the company of another woman and didn't seem to care much. I can't be married to someone like that."

"He's changed. His father's illness has made him see the error of his ways. He has grown as a man."

"So did he break up with the bimbo or did she break up with him?"

There is a short lapse of silence. "She is the one who ended the relationship."

"So he really hasn't learned all that much."

"He regrets losing you."

"With all due respect, I strongly disagree."

"Bam must grow up and take over his father's business. He is ready for the task. He will be giving up his polo career for the good of the family. That should give you an idea of the level of his sincerity and growth."

"I wish you all the best and will say a prayer for your husband. Thank you for calling, but I must go now."

I quickly hang up and walk into my house, shocked at the contrast of how it looks now compared to how it looked this morning.

It looks empty. Barren.

Like me.

But as I wander around, I start to see what Peyton saw. A house with stunning architectural details and character and, with all the formal furniture moved out, it already feels more like home than it ever has.

I nod my head, my mind and my heart coming together with one thought. I'm going to have a child—whether through adoption or surrogacy, it's time for me to pursue my options.

RILEY'S PENTHOUSE - L.A.

Riley

I GET A group text from Dallas that includes Keatyn.

> **Dallas:** *Front Door wants a face-to-face meeting with the three of us to hammer out the final details. I know you are filming, Keatyn, but could you meet tonight after?*
>
> **Keatyn:** *We're wrapping up now, so maybe 9?*
>
> **Me:** *Are you sure you're up for that? You've been going all day.*
>
> **Keatyn:** *I need food more than sleep right now. Can we have a late dinner?*
>
> **Dallas:** *I'll get us a private dining room at the usual place. See you soon.*

I send Ariela a quick text to let her know I have a late business meeting and that I'll call her after, and then I head to the restaurant. When I get off the elevator in the lobby, Shelby is just walking in the building.

"What are you doing here?"

"I needed to see you. You haven't called me since you said you'd find me a place to live."

"My assistant is working on it."

She frowns then looks down at the floor, her shoulders shaking.

"Why are you crying?" I ask.

"My roommate kicked me out of the apartment. She said if I can't pay my rent, I have to go. I have nowhere to go, Riley."

"I said I'd cover your rent. How much do you need?"

"It doesn't matter now. She already has someone new moving in. My stuff is all in my car. I don't know what to do. I've been poor before but never homeless. I can sleep in my car, but I need somewhere safe to park. Could I at least park here where it's safe?"

I close my eyes tightly, knowing I have no option. I put my arm around her and walk her to the elevator. "Come on. I'll take you upstairs. You can stay with me until Tyler finds you a new place."

She sobs into my chest. "Thank you. Thank you. I'm sorry I'm bothering you. I'm so embarrassed."

I hug her. I'd be a dick if I didn't offer her some comfort. "Why are you embarrassed?"

"For not having enough money to pay my rent. I never should have gone to those red carpet events with you. I was just so excited. Opportunities like that don't often happen to a girl like me."

"You're a sweet girl, Shelby. I've been fortunate that I've never had to worry about being able to pay my rent, but I imagine it's not pleasant."

"It's not."

"I'll have the valet park your car and bring up a few things that you might need for tonight. I have to go to a business meeting. I'm due there in ten minutes." I escort her to the guest bedroom. "Make yourself comfortable."

I expect her to say something about sleeping in my room, but she doesn't, and that makes me feel better. I know this isn't just a ploy to get with me.

"Do you have anything to eat here?" she asks timidly.

I grab some money out of my wallet and toss it on the coffee table. "There's a bunch of delivery menus in the drawer next to the fridge. Just give them my name, they should have the address."

"You eat take out a lot?" she asks.

"Sure. Why?"

"I just figured you went to fancy dinners every night."

"Hardly," I say with a chuckle. "I'll be back soon."

WHEN I GET to the meeting, Keatyn greets me with a hug.

I don't usually hug her back, but tonight I do.

"What was that for?" she asks.

"Shelby showed up at my place because she got kicked out of her apartment. I'm letting her stay with me until Tyler finds her somewhere to live."

"Why did she get kicked out?"

"Because she didn't have the money for rent."

"Riley, you're a good judge of character. How are you feeling about this girl?"

"She thought she was going to have to sleep in her car tonight. She didn't even ask to stay with me, just wanted a safe place to park and wondered if she could park in my garage."

"That's sad. So is she sleeping with you tonight?"

"I showed her the guest room and told her to put her stuff in there. She didn't argue."

"How's Tyler coming on the apartment search?"

"Honestly, I have no idea. Dallas and I spent most of the day going over all the details in this contract, then I stayed late to catch up on email."

"Call him," she says as a waiter brings her a glass of sparkling water and asks what I would like. I order a bottle of wine for the table then call Tyler.

AFTER GETTING AN update, I tell Keatyn, "He says the only place he's been able to find is a furnished unit in my building. I'm not sure I want her that close."

"You could always put her up at a hotel for the month. She'd probably enjoy it."

"Hmm. That's a good idea. Then if it is my baby, I'll buy her something permanent. I'll text Tyler and tell him to book a bungalow. It will be like a vacation for her."

"Is she still working?"

"Yeah, but she said she's been sick a lot."

"But you said that she works at a nightclub. Has she had morning sickness all day?"

"I don't know. Do you think she's lying? She seemed so upset about the apartment. Hell, I don't know what to do or think."

"I'd move her into a bungalow first thing in the morning," Keatyn says.

Dallas slaps me on the back, letting me know that he's arrived. He has the studio attorney and three other executives with him. Everyone exchanges pleasantries, and we get down to business.

THE NEGOTIATIONS GO smoothly on most points until the Captive Films name comes up.

"I'm hesitant to part with Captive," Keatyn says. "We've worked hard to develop the brand, and it's my understanding you are wanting just our assets."

"The brand is part of what we want to acquire," an executive for the other side says.

"And what about *The Keatyn Chronicles* trilogy? It's not addressed in the contract. When you put this deal together, the movie hadn't released yet. So we either pull it from the deal, or you adjust the value according-ly."

"Oh, I don't know about that," the attorney starts to say.

Keatyn looks the CEO straight in the eye. "Donny, you know what the box office numbers have been. And I know you know that industry experts are predicting the video and on-demand sales will be some of the best in movie history."

BY THE TIME we finally come to an agreement, it's close to midnight.

"That was grueling," Keatyn states, echoing my thoughts.

"I thought it was exhilarating," Dallas counters. "And it went amazingly well. We got almost everything we wanted. I think their CEO was starstruck. When you whipped out your smile on him, I thought he might pass out."

Keatyn laughs. "Don't be silly. I'm still on the fence

about the name, though. I don't think I can give it up."

"I thought you wanted to move on?"

"I do. I didn't think I'd be able to sell the rights to the trilogy, but what they offered was crazy high. We can't refuse that. And it's not like I can't watch it if I'm feeling nostalgic, right?"

"Plus, you're living your own fairytale, isn't that what you always say?" Dallas encourages.

She turns to me. "Riley, what do you think about the name?"

"I'm okay with it going. We'll come up with something new. Dallas has some good ideas."

"But Brooklyn named it," she says, tears gathering in her eyes.

"Why don't we all sleep on it?" I offer.

"Okay," she says, then she looks at her watch. "At least it's late. Maybe the paparazzi won't be outside. Things have been crazy since that article suggested I'm pregnant. Everyone wants some exclusive photo of my alleged baby bump. I've had to suck in my stomach all day. It's exhausting."

"So are you going to announce it soon?" I ask her.

"No, I'm not. Besides, it's not the first time that I've been pregnant," she makes quotes in the air, *with Knox's love child.*"

"That would piss me off if I were Aiden," Dallas says.

"It does, but I want him out of that kind of spotlight as much as possible. And if he ever said something they would twist it anyway. The tabloids want me and Knox together, because we sell magazines."

She meets up with her security detail, and we all

leave the restaurant together.

The amount of paparazzi and flashes of cameras catches me off guard.

"Keatyn, Keatyn! Is it true? Are you pregnant?" they shout.

She walks directly over to one of the reporters and gives him a dazzling smile, causing the cameras to click away.

"Give me a break, Jared," she says. "How many times has it been announced that I'm pregnant?"

Jared scrunches up his face.

"Exactly," she says.

"We were told you were having a meeting with First Door Films. Rumor has it that they want to acquire Captive."

"We can't comment on that," she says appropriately.

The reporter rolls his eyes but keeps trying. "I heard the *Trinity* filming is wrapping up this week. What's next for you?"

"I'm taking a three-week vacation then I'll be joining Knox and the crew in London to do the location shoots."

"Is this really the last *Trinity* movie?"

"That's the plan."

He squints at her. "But it sounds like you're leaving the door open."

"Knox and I will always leave the door open for the right script."

"And do you have a script in mind?"

"Not for *Trinity*," she says, walking away toward her waiting car.

"Wait, what are you saying?" he yells, following her.

She turns around before getting into the car. "I'm saying I'm pretty positive this won't be my last movie with Knox, but it *is* the last *Trinity* movie."

"Oh my stars! Did you sign on to do another project together? Why haven't we heard about this?"

"Because nothing can be announced at the moment," she teases, then pulls me into the car even though I wasn't planning on riding with her.

ONCE WE'RE SAFELY in the car, I ask her, "How do you do that? You and Knox can both twist whatever they say and turn it around on them."

"I know what they want to hear," she shrugs.

"What do they want to hear?"

"Big news, Riley. But I don't want to talk about that. You and I need to discuss giving up the Captive name. I thought I could do it, but I can't. They want our assets, not the name. That was obvious based on what they upped the offer to."

"Is that the reason you practically kidnapped me just now?"

"Yes, Riley, it is. Could you really just let the name Brooklyn chose go to someone who doesn't care about it?"

"We have the Brooklyn Wright Marine Biology Memorial Fund. We sponsor up-and-coming surfers on the pro tour in his honor. It's not like we're just going to forget about him."

"Riley, I left the majority of what really happened to Brooklyn out of the movie. You know that. He went through a lot because of me."

"No, he went through a lot because of Vincent. It's not your fault that Vincent tortured him to find out where you were."

"I know it's not, but even after Vincent beat him . . . even after he was threatened with a loaded gun to his head. And even after Vincent broke two of his fingers, he never told. The name of our company is the only thing—besides my surfboard, my tattoo, and a book of poetry—that I have left of him."

I give her a hug. "And maybe it's time that you got over the guilt and let it go. Maybe giving up the name will be freeing for you. It's a constant reminder of that pain. That can't be healthy, now that I think about it. Think about all the good things you can do with this money. Not to mention setting up your children and your children's children for life."

She sighs. "Yeah, I suppose you're right. Aiden said the same thing, but . . ."

"I will think about it tonight. I promise," I say reassuringly.

"Thanks, Riley," she says, kissing my cheek and telling me goodnight as the driver pulls up to my building.

I stop before going in, sit on a mahogany bench out front, and call Ariela. I don't want to talk to her in front of Shelby.

ASHER VINEYARDS – SONOMA COUNTY

Ariela

I SMILE AS one of the photos I took during homecoming of Riley's handsome face pops up on the screen of my phone, indicating a call from him.

"Hey, Kitty," he says, causing certain parts of my female anatomy to warm.

"Hey, yourself. How was your meeting?"

"It went pretty well. We're negotiating to sell most of Captive Films."

"Really? Will you still have a job?"

"After this deal, I won't need a job, but I'll still work. I'm going back to doing what I love—producing."

"That's amazing, Riley. I'm happy for you."

"Aiden told me that they offered you a job."

"Yeah, they did, but I don't know if I'll accept."

"Is it something you would like to do?"

"Oh my gosh, are you kidding me? The ability to design my own venue? Every single venue I've ever worked at, I've thought about how I could make it better. And couples are so into personalizing their weddings, to be able to create spaces that would allow them to do that in an elegant way would be so cool."

"Then I think you should take them up on it."

"But the job would be here, Riley," she says softly.

"What if I told you that I'm thinking it's time I put down some roots of my own. I would love to have a place on this coast that's big like my parents' place in the Hamptons. Somewhere all the kids could come. Where we could all spend the holidays together."

"Your family would love that. Would you keep your place in L.A?"

"I think so. I would assume I will still be here often for business."

"So you'd go on location to produce?"

"Okay, so this is a secret, but Keatyn and Knox are going to build a small studio in the area. Knox already bought a house near Asher Vineyards, and he and Keatyn bought the land near it that includes large outbuildings to use as sets. She wants to spend more time there. Her and Aiden want to start a family."

"Aiden mentioned this afternoon that the tabloids are speculating she's pregnant."

"Well, that's pretty normal for her. Of course, they all want Knox to be the father." I laugh. "It's really kind of crazy."

"Sounds like it. Which is probably why she'd like to be here. It's so peaceful and beautiful. And it smells so good."

"How is the wedding planning coming?"

"Really good. Oh, I forgot to tell you. I hired an assistant."

"That was fast."

"He flew out this morning."

"From where?"

"Don't laugh, but he worked at the coffee shop, and he hit on me, and then he went to see the trilogy with me."

"He hit on you?"

"Yeah, but he's harmless. I mean, I think, mostly. He's young and cute. Honestly, his cockiness reminded me of you in high school."

"You liked me in high school."

"No, Riley. I loved you. Speaking of that," I say. "Have you read the note?"

"The note?"

"Yeah, the one I gave you at homecoming? I sort of expected you'd say something about it."

"Shit, I totally forgot about it."

"Can you read it now?"

"Uh, sure, let me get it out of my wallet."

I hear some rustling then he says, "It's in pink marker. Just like all the other notes you wrote me." He hesitates. "Ariela, we put the past behind us. I'm not sure I should read this."

"I really want you to. Tonight. Now. I need you to know."

"Okay, here goes—

"Riley-

I've wanted to talk to you about this for weeks, but I just couldn't.

I love you so much. And I wish I could go to California and become your wife.

But, I can't.

Because if I do, it will hurt my dad.

No matter what I choose, someone is going to get hurt.

And no matter what I choose, I know that I'll be the one who will hurt the most. Because none of this is what I want.

What I want, if I'm being completely honest,

71

is three things.

I want to be able to live out my dream of going to Princeton.
I want to marry you.
And I want my parents to be proud of me.

So I've decided to go to Princeton.
If I do that, I'll have two out of the three things that I want.
I hope and pray that you will understand. That you will still love me. That you will still want to marry me. That we can figure out a way to have a long-distance relationship. That we can stay together until I graduate and come to California with you.
I love you, Riley.
I know in my heart you are the only boy I will ever love.
You've held my heart captive since the day we met.
Please tell me that we can work this out.
That it won't be the end of us.

All my love forever,
Ariela"

He's quiet for a moment, and I wonder what he's thinking. Maybe it was a mistake letting him read it after all these years, but I desperately needed him to know that I never wanted us to be over. Ever.

"Are you fucking kidding me? You've had this note all this time? Why didn't you mail it to me? Send it to Keatyn? Message me on Facebook? You ruined us, and this note would have changed everything. Showing it to me now, this is just—cruel."

"But I thought it would make you feel better knowing that I never wanted us to end."

"Yeah, well it doesn't. It makes it ten times worse. Look, I don't know if I can do this. Go through all of this again. It's late. I have to go."

Then he hangs up on me.

RILEY'S PENTHOUSE - L.A.

Riley

I'M PISSED OFF when I step into my elevator and make my way up.

What the fuck was I thinking?

I can't do this with Ariela.

I can't keep dredging this shit up.

It's just not going to work. I don't need all week to figure out what I'm going to tell her at the wedding. I know what I'm going to say. *Fuck this. And fuck you.*

I'm pulling off my tie when I walk into my bedroom and find Shelby hoisted up in a swing on the bathroom door, wearing nothing but a pair of black, studded leather panties.

Oh yeah, this is exactly what I need right now.

I don't say a word, just shed my clothes and do her every which way.

AS I'M DOZING off, exhausted from both the kinky sex

73

and the emotion of the day, a sentence floats through my brain. *You've held my heart captive since the day we met.*

My eyes open with a start, and I sit up, grab my phone, and call Dallas' number in a panic.

When he answers groggily, I blurt out, "We can't sell the name."

"But at dinner you were all for it."

"I promised Keatyn that I would think about it. She doesn't want to change the name because of Brooklyn."

"I miss him too, and I understand he thought up the name but—"

"I lied to her. Told her all the things she needed to hear. I had no intention of thinking about it anymore. My mind was made up. I was going to tell her the same thing this morning. That we should sell it."

"What changed your mind?"

"Fate, maybe?"

"You're going to have to be a little more specific."

"When Ariela broke up with me on graduation day, she intended to put a note on my car. Instead, she ran into me and blurted it all out then ran off and forgot to give me the note. She's kept it all this time though and gave it to me this past weekend. With the party and then our rush to get home for the baby's birth, I had forgotten about it. Tonight she made me read it."

"And that has to do with our deal, how?"

"One of the lines in her note was that I've held her heart captive since the day we met. It's a sign, Dallas. And I don't really believe in signs."

"It's going to mean less money," he says with a sigh

that lets me know he won't fight us on this.

"I think Keatyn will be okay with that. This is more important to her. And, really, it should be more important to us. It's where we started. It's only fitting that when we start over the name is part of it. It's part of us, Dallas."

"You gonna start crying about this?"

"No, but it does make me emotional."

Dallas sounds choked up when he replies. "It makes me emotional too. I'll take it off the table. You call Keatyn and tell her the news—at a reasonable hour."

SHELBY ROLLS OVER, pushing her tits against my chest. "Ariela was your high school girlfriend? she asks. "Are you still in love with her?"

"Obviously not," I say, running my hand across her nipple and feeling both it and myself harden.

"Again, daddy?" she giggles.

"Yes, again."

TUESDAY, OCTOBER 14TH
RILEY'S PENTHOUSE - L.A.

Riley

I WAKE UP to the smell of bacon. I roll over and glance at the clock. Shit! It's almost eight!

Although it shouldn't be that big of a surprise. I was fucking Shelby until at least four this morning.

I drag myself out of bed, quickly shower, and get dressed.

"Well, look at you," Shelby says, when I join her in the kitchen. "There's just something so sexy about a man in a suit."

I grab her around the waist, pulling her close. "And there's something pretty sexy about a woman cooking me breakfast naked."

She giggles. "I thought you'd like that, daddy."

Although it used to make me cringe when she called me that, it's honestly starting to grow on me. I take the spatula out of her hand and spank her ass with it.

"Oh! Yeah. You know I like it like that," she says,

bending over. "Do it again."

I smack her again, harder this time. She flips around, unzips my pants, and drops to her knees, taking my dick in her mouth and expertly sucking it. I lean back against the kitchen counter and think *this* is the life of Riley Johnson.

And I fucking love it.

Especially when I pick her up, set her on the counter, and drive the point home.

AFTER A THOROUGH fucking, she finishes cooking breakfast and presents it to me on a plate. "I'm going to make you breakfast every morning before you go to work."

But Riley Johnson doesn't do *every morning*. "Today you'll be moving into a bungalow."

"You mean after last night I don't get to stay here?"

"I'm a bachelor and set in my ways, Shelby. I need my space."

"But—"

"Have you ever seen a bungalow at Chateau Marmont?"

"*That's* the kind of bungalow you're talking about? Oh my God! I've heard about those!"

"So do you think you'd be okay staying there until we can find you a suitable place to live?"

She frowns and hangs her head. "They're really expensive, Riley. I don't need anything that nice. Besides, I don't have anything to wear to a place like that."

I push her chin up. "Then it sounds like you'll need to go shopping first."

"Riley, I can't . . ."

"I'll take care of it."

"Are you trying to get rid of me?" She starts crying. "I'm sorry, Riley. I'm just so emotional right now. Must be all the pregnancy hormones."

"Speaking of that, I thought you told me you've been sick?"

"I have been. I threw up first thing this morning. I usually feel okay until about midday then I'm exhausted."

"Are you still planning to work?"

Her eyes get big, and she looks at me like I'm nuts. "Of course I am, Riley. I appreciate that you're going to put me up and all, but I know how men are. As soon as they've used you up, they move on. And if you decide to move on, I'd be fucked. I'm not stupid."

"I'd say I'm not like other men, but I probably am. I work hard. I fuck a lot of women. It's who I am."

"I don't care about any of that, Riley. You know, sexually, I'm pretty open-minded. But just to be clear, if you're going to fuck around, so am I."

"I understand," I tell her, appreciating her candor. "Tyler, my assistant, will get in touch with you this morning. He'll have a personal shopper work with you and then get you all checked in."

"Will you come help me christen my new place tonight?"

"I'll try," I tell her, not wanting to commit, but knowing I'll be there with fucking bells on.

CAPTIVE FILMS – SANTA MONICA

Dawson

I TOOK THE girls to the airport this morning and got them on a plane back home.

It was not fun.

Harlow hung on me and cried, saying that she didn't want to leave. That she didn't care if Ava liked the school. That she wanted to be with her daddy and her soon-to-be-adopted pony.

I'm not sure what to do. Harlow loved the school when they visited yesterday. She and Carder seem thick as thieves, and I know if she came here, she'd do well. But she's more easygoing like me.

Ava is tougher. She said she had a good day, but that she didn't know yet if she wanted to move. My mom says it's because she's almost a teenager. That they are moody and don't know what they want. She says at some point, I'm just going to have to tell her she's moving, and that's it.

But I don't think she's right. Ava is a lot like her mother. She knows what she wants and is not afraid to go for it. Where Harlow is reckless abandon, Ava is a well-orchestrated plan. I think if I back off, she'll come to the right decision.

I blink away my thoughts and focus on the marketing calendar in front of me.

Tyler's voice comes over the speaker. "Keatyn is on line three."

"Hey, Keatyn," I say, picking up the receiver. "What's up?"

"I have some news I need to share with you. This is top secret, okay? We're calling a special board meeting this week, where we will announce the sale of Captive to Front Door Films."

"Oh, wow," I say, shocked. I know how these things work. When one company sells to another, most of the executives are fired. And that means me. "I probably wouldn't have come out here had I known."

"Most of the employees will have the option of taking a buyout or moving with the sale."

"I see." Shit, what are the girls going to say when I tell them I'm coming home?

"Riley and I want you to run our new company."

"Run it?"

"Yes, it will be a much smaller Captive Films. One that only takes on a few special projects at a time. We'll be taking *Daddy's Angel* with us, along with all my scripts that haven't been optioned by Captive—which is everything that's not currently in production. And Knox and I have a project in the works that we hope to run through the new Captive, as well."

"What's Riley going to do?"

"Produce movies. It's what he loves. Really, this sale will allow us all to get back to doing what we love. What we started out doing. Things won't be quite so hectic, you know?"

"That sounds nice, actually."

"How did the girls' visit go yesterday?"

"Harlow loved the school and is ready to move. Ava isn't so sure."

"She's at a hard age. I'm sure she doesn't want to leave her friends. Have you tried bribing her?"

I laugh. "That's the other reason Harlow is so gung-ho about California. She wants a pony, and Vanessa said she could adopt one of hers."

"Vanessa must really want you to stay."

"She's redoing her whole house. The girls seem to affect her. She showed us a playroom that she's kept locked up and told me about how she can't have more children."

"She *what?*"

"You didn't know?"

"No. Oh my gosh. No wonder she took the miscarriage so hard. I thought it was because of Bam's cheating but—oh, it all makes more sense now."

"Don't tell her I told you. I shouldn't have said anything. I didn't mean to betray her confidence. I assumed since you are best friends that you knew."

"I won't tell her, Dawes. So, back to your new job. I guess the first question is, would you be interested in being the CEO of a smaller, more nimble Captive Films?"

"I definitely would be."

"Good to hear. I should also mention that when this deal goes through, all of our employee stock in the company will vest and be paid out. If you recall, you received numerous shares as a sign-on bonus. I don't know if you would be interested, but if you would like to use those funds to buy into the new Captive, we'd love to take you on as a partner."

"Who all is investing? Will you still have a board to report to?"

"The investors are me, Riley, Dallas, and Knox. There won't be an outside board of directors. Basically, the plan is for you and Dallas and, hopefully, Tyler, to run the business with a small staff. We'll outsource anything else. We expect *Daddy's Angel* to be huge, and the project Knox and I will do next could win Captive its first Oscar. So what do you think?"

"Providing Ava agrees to come to school out here, I'm in."

"Anything I can do to help with that?"

"What do girls her age want?"

"When we were all up at the vineyard, she told Fallon that you won't let her wear makeup. I remember RiAnne saying it was a really big deal for Fallon this year."

"She's too young to wear makeup!"

"She doesn't want to wear a face full. Just tinted lip gloss and a little clear mascara."

"That's it?"

"That's what Fallon wears to school."

"*Makeup*? Could it be that simple?"

"Probably. Good luck."

I text Ava, knowing she has Wi-Fi on the plane.

Me: *I don't know how you feel about this, but Keatyn told me that in L.A. girls your age get to wear a little bit of makeup to school. Just a little. Like some of that lip stuff and a little mascara. You know I won't let you wear it now, but if you come to school here, I've decided you can.*

Ava: *Are you joking? Like, are you laughing out loud right now?*

Me: *No.*

Ava: *!!!!!!!!!!!!!!!*

Me: *What does that mean?*

Ava: *Just so I'm clear—we're talking black mascara, lipstick, blush, and glitter powder?*

Me: *Clear mascara, lip gloss, and glitter powder. I'll even throw in Instagram.*

Ava: *Really? Um, how about clear mascara, lip gloss, glitter powder, Instagram, and Snapchat?*

Me: *Instagram only and you have a deal.*

Ava: *Then I'd like to move to California with you and go to the school we visited. (And I might want to adopt a pony too.)*

Me: *Don't push your luck.*

Ava: *I love you, Daddy.*

Me: *I love you too, Ave.*

SHELBY'S BUNGALOW - SUNSET BLVD.

I PLOP DOWN on the couch in my hillside bungalow and call my former roommate. "Marcy, you're never going to believe where I am."

"I know where I am. At work."

"You have to get off and come over here."

"Where are you? Let me guess. Sugar Daddy kicked you out, and you need my help?"

"Nope. I'm sitting in a hillside bungalow at *the* Chateau Marmont. It's where I will be living for the next month. Go home, put on the classiest thing you own, and get over here. There are rich men everywhere! You can meet one. And I worked with a personal shopper today and got a shit ton of fancy clothes, not to mention getting my hair and makeup done. You probably won't even recognize me. I look totally classy."

"You looked pretty for those premieres."

"Yeah, but not like this. I look like a lady. I look like I *belong* here."

"Reality check, Shelby. In a month, he's going to find out he's not your baby daddy, and you're going to be out on your ass. Then what are you going to do?"

"Get your ass over here, and I'll tell you all the dirty details. Because after last night, there's no way he's kicking me out."

I SEE MY personal butler point Marcy in my direction poolside, where I'm sitting in the shade wearing a black one-piece swimsuit with a long, sheer cover-up and oversized Dolce & Gabbana sunglasses.

She walks right by me.

I grin to myself as she takes another lap.

When she comes back by me again, I discreetly say her name.

She turns and looks at me in shock, slowly sitting down.

"Your hair! What did they do to it?"

"The stylist said I shouldn't be bleaching. That my natural honey color is more flattering. What do you think?"

"You look like a Kardashian!"

"Oh my God! Do you think? Maybe I should start building my social media presence now. I'll call it *The Bungalow Life*."

"That's actually a really good idea. Those bloggers

make big bucks. So tell me why you're here and not with Riley. If you ask me, it's a step backwards."

"Except for the fact that we fucked ten ways to Sunday last night."

"I thought he was in love with the preppy girl?"

I shrug. "What can I say? I'm good."

"Tell me what you did!"

"When he came home, I was mounted up in one of those over-the-door swings. They aren't as fun as the ones that hang from the ceiling, but it served its purpose."

"What were you wearing?"

"That black leather thong with the spiked studs on it. Nothing else."

"What man can resist an invitation like that?"

"None that I know," I agree.

The butler comes to stand in front of the table. "Miss Stanford, is there anything I can get you?"

"Do you have a menu or something?" Marcy asks.

"We have a menu, but our bungalow guests can order whatever they are in the mood for."

"You got any corndogs?" Marcy asks. I glare at her. "Just kidding."

"I'd love a grilled chicken salad, Fred," I say, "and a bottle of champagne, please."

"Ditto," Marcy says rudely.

In that moment, I realize I won't be inviting Marcy back. I survey the women gathered around the pool and decide I'm going to learn to act like I'm one of them and not act like my beer-guzzling, corn-dog-eating friend.

I also realize that she's the only one who knows that

I'm not pregnant with Riley's baby.

And that could prove to be a problem.

"So IF YOU could do anything—and money was no object—what would you do?" I ask her after she's downed three glasses of champagne.

"I'd go back to Michigan and open my own nail salon. That's what I went to school for. Thought I'd come to L.A. and make a ton of money doing nails. Could never get on at one of those ritzy salons."

"Hmm, what do you think something like that would cost?"

"Believe it or not, I know the answer to that question. Eleven thousand dollars. I'm saving for it."

"How much you got?"

"About eight hundred," she says with a sad laugh.

"If you had enough money, would you leave all the sunshine and go home?"

"In a heartbeat," she says wistfully. "I miss the seasons. My family thinks I work at one of those ritzy places and that I'm learning how to run one. I can't go back until I have the money to do what I said I would do." She looks at her watch. "Damn, I have to catch a cab. I picked up a double and need to be back to work in thirty minutes."

"I'll walk you out."

As SOON AS she leaves, I go back to my room and call Riley.

"Are you almost done for the day? I'm lonely."

"Lonely? I heard you shopped all day and were at the salon."

"Maybe I'm just horny."

"Well, that changes things."

"Does that mean you're on your way?"

"No, I have a meeting tonight. If I come, it will be later."

"Riley, do you ever loan people money?"

"Sometimes, why?"

"Would you lend me eleven thousand dollars?"

"What for?"

"A friend. She wants to open a nail salon back home in Michigan. She waits tables and has been saving for over three years, but with the way things are going she'll never have enough. Never mind, Riley. It's stupid of me to ask. I just had the most amazing day, but I feel really guilty about it."

"Why do you feel guilty?"

"Did you give the personal shopper a budget?"

"Yeah."

"Was it eleven thousand dollars?"

"Actually, it was ten."

"We spent eleven, and I was just thinking it's crazy. Eleven thousand dollars for some clothes and shoes when that kind of money would change her life. Would you be mad at me if I took it all back and gave her the money?"

"Keep the clothes, Shelby. Call Tyler with your bank information, and I'll have him wire you the money, and you can write your friend a check."

"Really?"

"Yeah, really. It's sweet of you to want to do that. You surprise me. In a good way. In fact, why don't I cancel my meeting and take you out for dinner tonight?

If we're going to raise a baby together, I'd like to learn more about you."

"Can we eat at the bar here at the hotel? I've heard it's, like, legendary."

"Of course we can. I'll have Tyler make the arrangements."

I hang up the phone feeling giddy. Everything is going to work out perfectly.

And the truth is, even though I am lying to him about the baby, I wasn't lying when I said I love him.

I look around my posh room. I mean, what's not to love?

CAPTIVE FILMS – SANTA MONICA

IT'S GETTING LATE, and I haven't heard from Vanessa all day, so I call her.

"How's the redecorating going?"

"It's kind of crazy here. Would you like to come over and see my empty house?"

"Is it completely empty? Not even a bed?"

"Do we really need a bed?" she asks, her voice low and sultry.

"Probably not. I'm finished up here. Shall I head that way?"

"Yes. I miss you."

WHEN I ARRIVE, Vanessa greets me at the door,

wrapped in a sheer robe and nothing else.

"I've missed you." My lips crash into hers as I pick her up and carry her into the bedroom. All that's there is a mattress on the floor.

It's all we need.

"DAMN," SHE SAYS, stroking my arm with the back of her hand. "I'm going to have to make you miss me more often."

"No way. We're too good together not to do this every single day."

"Unless you move back home," she says with a pout. And God, can those lips form the most perfect pout.

"I have good news on that front. The girls decided to move here. I need to finalize it with the school, but they will be here full-time soon."

Her face breaks into a wide smile. "Speaking of that," she says. "I know it's maybe a little soon for this, but what would you think about you and the girls moving in with me?"

"Really?" I ask, curling my hand around the back of her neck and tasting those lips once again.

"Is that a *good* really or an *I can't believe she asked me that* really?"

"Well, your house is closer to the girls' school than mine is. It'd save us commute time."

She gives me a playful smack. "Not funny."

"Vanessa, I'd love to move in with you. And I think the girls would love it."

"You don't think it's too soon?"

"Do you love me?" I ask her.

"I do."

"Do you plan on loving me for a long time?"

She smiles. "I do."

"Then the answer is yes."

"Do you think the girls will be okay with it?"

"I think the girls will be nuts about it. Are you kidding? Harlow can see her adopted pony every day. And Ava would be closer to her friends. Don't Dallas and RiAnne live nearby?"

"Only a few blocks away."

I look at the ceiling. "How long before the house is ready?"

"It will be done by the time we get back from the wedding. It would be fun to have you move in with me."

I nod. I know it sounds crazy but it feels right. "Can we redo a couple rooms just for the girls?"

"I'm already ahead of you."

I give her a long kiss then a little smack on the butt. "Let's get dressed, go out, and celebrate tonight."

"That sounds fun." She grabs my hand. "Come in my closet and help me pick out something to wear."

I follow her gorgeous, naked body through her bathroom and into an expansive closet. *Closet* is probably the wrong word for it. This is like a garage for clothes.

"This is huge," I stutter, peeking in.

"It's the one area of the house that I didn't want to change."

"Why's that?"

"Because this dressing room was designed just to my taste. The pale pink on the wall is soft and relaxing and makes my skin look glowing. The soft grey cabinets remind me of my favorite cashmere sweater."

"And the chandeliers?"

She grins. "Diamonds, of course. Come inside."

"I feel like I'm walking into a vault."

"That's because you just did. This room is temperature and humidity controlled and can lock from the inside or out. That pretty wooden door we walked through is pure steel underneath."

"Please tell me you have never uttered the words *I don't have anything to wear,*" I say, taking in the rows and rows of clothing.

She laughs. "Believe it or not, I have. When I went to Bam's polo matches, I was expected to wear haute couture at all times and could never be seen in the same thing twice."

"What's this?" I ask, pointing to another door.

"If someone managed to get in here, they'd still have to crack this safe to get to my jewels."

"Your jewels?"

"Yes," she says, keying in a code and then opening the door to a room that looks like it belongs in a royal palace. Behind glass cases are displays of jewels like I have never seen before.

"These look like they should be on exhibit somewhere."

"I'm thinking of auctioning them off, honestly."

"Do you like them?" I stupidly ask. Any woman's answer would be a resounding yes.

"Some of them are very pretty."

"How does someone afford this?"

"I told you, Bam's family is quite wealthy. They

own diamond, gemstone, and granite mines. Among other things."

"Wow," I say, looking at a large green stone.

"That one is uncut," she says. "A gift from his father on our wedding day, to be turned into something spectacular on our tenth anniversary, which obviously we never made it to. Would it offend you if I wore any of these when I was with you?"

"The fur didn't bother me," I say, starting to recover from the dazzling sparkle. "Although, obviously I wouldn't want you to wear your wedding ring."

"I love that about you, Dawson. You're so strong and confident."

Confident, maybe, I think. But nuts. What am I doing here? I look down at my empty ring finger, knowing I finally stopped wearing my own wedding ring just a few months ago when Keatyn first offered me the job.

I look around at everything in the closet. Think of the wealth this room represents. I think of where I just came from—living with my parents, not a dime to my name. I could never begin to think a woman like Vanessa could truly love me forever. I couldn't give her anything.

Except for my heart.

Which sucks, because she's somehow already managed to acquire it.

I sit down on a fur chaise, feeling defeated. This closet is the epitome of luxury spending. She was right when she told me that's what she planned to major in.

Because she sure as hell did.

I had done well, but not to this level well. Between

my salary and my trust fund, we could have lived comfortably for the rest of our lives.

Until . . .

I shake my head, willing away the thought.

Vanessa chooses a necklace—one that is probably worth over a million dollars—and a sexy black dress and is getting dressed when her butler interrupts us.

"Miss Vanessa, you have a caller," he says then retreats.

"It must be Peyton. She mentioned coming over tonight. I haven't checked my phone."

I throw my suit back on and follow her into the entry, where an elegantly dressed man stands holding a massive bouquet of red roses.

"Bam!" Vanessa says. "What are you doing here?"

He hands the butler the roses then opens up a box. Inside is a ruby. A massive glittering ruby about the size of her fist.

"This is for you, my darling."

Vanessa's eyes get huge, and she puts her dainty hand over her mouth to hide her shock, but it's clear she's impressed.

I take a moment to size Bam up. If this were a bar room brawl, I'd kick his ass for sure. He's a good five inches shorter than me and lean compared to my bulk.

But this isn't about that. His clothes, his shoes, even his attitude reeks of money and privilege in a way I never have, and my family is far from poor.

He takes a few steps forward and pulls Vanessa into his arms.

And she looks good there.

They look like a raven-haired billionaire Barbie and

Ken.

"Bam, this is Dawson," Vanessa says, pulling away and introducing me. "We, um, work together."

We *work* together. Not *we're fucking*. Not *we're dating*. Not *we're in love*. Not *I just asked him and his daughters to move in with me*.

Well, fuck this.

"I have to go," I say suddenly. "Nice to meet you, Bam. I'll leave you two to catch up. See you at *work* tomorrow, Vanessa."

Then I get the hell out of there before she can stop me.

Not that she'd even want to.

VANESSA'S ESTATE - HOLMBY HILLS
Vanessa

I SEE THE hurt in Dawson's eyes when I introduce him as someone I work with, and I'm not that surprised when he leaves.

I don't want him to leave, but I also don't want Bam to know about Dawson. If he thinks he has competition, it will only up the stakes for him. Bam gets what Bam wants.

He always has.

The massive ruby glinting from the box in front of me is just one example of how he manipulates. It's hard for a woman to think with all that sparkle so close.

"Now that your work is done, we must talk," Bam

says, escorting me to the living room.

He looks around, realizing all the furniture is gone. "Where is everything?"

"I'm doing some redecorating. It's out in the garage right now. When we got divorced, you only asked for your personal belongings. Is there anything in the house that you want before I get rid of it?"

He smiles at me, bringing his hand to my face. "There is only but one thing I, Juan Fabio Martinez, want. And that, my darling, is you."

"I heard you got dumped by the supermodel."

"She is young, not ready to settle down," he says, ignoring the *dumped* part.

"And you are?"

"I need a woman. You are the only girl I have ever truly loved. If you will allow me another chance, I will swear my undying love to you."

"You did that twice already, it didn't take."

"There will be no other women, Vanessa. Of that I give you my oath."

Bam is very sexy. Women all over the world desire him. There are websites dedicated to his folly both on and off the polo field. His sexy accent combined with his deep voice speaking the words I longed to hear give me pause.

How could they not? I loved him for most of my life, and after we broke up these are the exact words I needed to hear. Dreamed of hearing. That he would realize he needed me. Wanted me. That he made a mistake. That he didn't desire anyone but me. And to hear these words now . . .

"My father is dying, and I have also vowed to my

family to stop my philandering ways. It is my time to take over his empire, an endeavor with great responsibility."

I don't reply, so he continues.

"As proof of my seriousness, I will be announcing my retirement from polo to the world very soon, and I need you by my side, my darling Vanessa."

"I don't mean to be rude, Bam, but you were having sex with someone else while I was in the hospital losing our child."

He dismisses my comment with a wave of his hand. "The past is the past. I cannot change what is there. I can only hope to repair my life so that our future is bright. The loss of our child cut me deeply. I regret not being there, and I've had to live with that decision. I am like my father, my mother says—raging hormones, too many for one woman—but she is wrong. I want to make it up to you. I want to have heirs with you. I was surprised by your pregnancy before."

"We'd been married for quite some time. I told you I was ready to have a baby. You didn't disagree."

"That's because I wanted for you to have everything your heart desired. That is still my wish. What do you want, Vanessa? Homes across the world? A new yacht? To be dripping in gold and jewels? Whatever you ask for, my darling, I will present to you on a diamond encrusted platter."

"What I want is to understand why you did what you did."

"Mentally—emotionally—I wasn't there yet. Not ready for responsibility. Not ready to settle down. I am like a wild mare in my youth. I had to be broken."

"And you're broken now?" I ask, not able to help adding an eye roll. "The model dumping you did that?"

"I understand your reluctance," he says, taking my hand. "Can we go sit down somewhere, have a bottle of wine, and discuss this?"

"Sure, let's go outside." I call to my butler, Bernard, "Can you please bring us a bottle of—"

"The Chateau Margaux, please," he says, interrupting me.

"I thought we weren't supposed to drink that," I counter. "Isn't that the hundred thousand dollar limited collector's edition?"

"It is, but this is a very special occasion, my darling. Our reunion is worth celebrating."

"Bam, we're not getting back together."

He leads me outside, his hand fitting into the small of my back and reminding me of so many occasions in ballrooms, private clubs, and restaurants around the world when I was so in love with him. When the luxury and royalty of it all was new. When I didn't know the consequences of his love.

We sit in silence until our wine is brought.

After sniffing, swirling, and tasting, Bam declares the wine good enough to drink, so Bernard pours us each a glass.

Once he has retreated and we are left alone in an uncomfortable silence, Bam raises his glass to mine.

"Tonight we drink a wine that is considered by many to be priceless. I, myself, used to believe that it was, but I have learned the hard way that the only thing priceless in life, is love. Salud."

When our glasses touch, I see the pain behind

Bam's smile.

"I will be honest with you, Vanessa."

"That's always nice," I say, trying to keep the sarcasm out of my voice.

"My father's illness was unexpected. Until I was called upon to provide for my family, I did not have so much responsibility. I was but a boy playing a man's game. Now, it is my time. I want to renew our vows. I will shower you with gifts and attention. We will have children. As many as you want. I pledge to be a good father. Our children will have everything. I know you need more than my words. You need proof. I will spend the rest of my life proving this to you."

He pulls another box out from his jacket pocket, opens it to reveal a diamond that belongs in a museum, and gets down on one knee.

"Do you remember those weekends on my yacht when we were young? How crazy in love we were when we secretly wed. Darling, I've loved you since I learned how to love. Will you do me the vast honor of marrying me again?"

Tears fill my eyes as emotions overcome me.

VANESSA'S ESTATE – HOLMBY HILLS

AFTER I BEELINE out the door, jump into the Ferrari I couldn't have bought for myself, and drive off, I'm both pissed at myself for leaving and pissed at her for letting me go.

I know Keatyn is working late tonight, so I call Aiden. "Hey, you in town?"

"Yeah, just got back. What's up?"

"Wanna go get a drink or something?"

"Why don't you just come here. I can't really leave tonight."

That's a good idea, I think. I'll drop the car off at home and walk down. Then I can drink.

And drink.

"Is Keatyn home?"

"No, not yet. You'll see why I can't leave when you get here."

"I'll be there shortly."

"Are you okay? he asks.

"I don't know," I reply.

AIDEN GREETS ME with a pile of yellow fur cradled in his arms, a pale pink ribbon around its neck.

When I talk, the puppy looks up at me, licks my fingers, then yawns, and tucks its head back into Aiden's arms.

"You got a dog?"

"Yeah, Keatyn and I always talked about getting a golden retriever and since she's decided to slow down with work and spend more time at the vineyard, it finally seemed like the right time. I'm going to surprise her tonight."

"You've always given Keatyn thoughtful gifts," I say, following him to the bar in the kitchen.

"Well, I try to make them meaningful. I mean, any guy can shower a girl with jewels and expensive gifts."

"Not any guy," I mutter.

"Can you do the honors, so I don't have to put her down? She whines if I don't hold her when she sleeps," he says.

"Already got you wrapped around her paw? Wait until you have a child." I pour us each a glass of scotch.

Aiden beams.

"What's the smile for?"

"We're expecting."

"You are? Wow. Congratulations, man. There is nothing in the world that compares to holding your baby." I think about my girls, knowing there aren't enough diamonds in the world—let alone Vanessa's closet—that would ever mean as much as they do. "Children are the ultimate jewel."

"I can't wait to experience that," Aiden says, rubbing the puppy's head. "Although, I will admit I'm a little nervous."

"Just spend a lot of time with them and always let them know they are loved. They will turn out beautifully."

"Says the guy who's already been through the sleepless nights and the terrible twos," he says with a laugh.

"You'll survive and forget how terrible it was. Now, I'm starting to have to worry about boys. And slumber parties. And mean girls. And soon, I'll have to deal with them getting their periods."

Aiden takes a drink and shakes his head, looking overwhelmed.

"One step at a time," I tell him.

"So, you seemed upset when you called."

"I was at Vanessa's. Have you ever seen her closet?"

"No, but I've heard about it. Jewels, expensive paintings."

"You mean that Monet was real?"

"Yep."

"Holy shit." I run my hands though my hair and pour myself another drink.

"What's wrong?"

"She has everything. And I mean *everything*. Her ex came to her house tonight and pulled out a ruby the size of her fucking fist. I can't compete with that shit. I can't afford that lifestyle. I can't give her anything like that."

"Do you think she expects it?"

"You know what happened, Aiden."

"Dawson, what do you like about Vanessa?"

"She's amazing. Sweet. Sincere. Soft. Confident. I love her red lips and how she looks equally sexy in high heels and bare feet."

"Not once in that list did you mention a single materialistic thing," he comments. "You and Vanessa are sort of opposite in that respect."

"How so?"

"Whitney left you with no money, but with something more important."

"My girls."

"Exactly. And Bam left Vanessa with more money that she knows what to do with, but without the one thing she wanted."

"She came over the other night wearing nothing but a fur coat he gave her. She used to hate the coat."

"Probably because it was something he gave her to make up for being an asshole. He was always trying to buy her love instead of trying to earn it."

I study Aiden, knowing I don't need to say it, but that I should. "I watched the movies before I went to work at Captive."

"*The Keatyn Chronicles?*"

"Yeah, and I've never really apologized for being such a dick to you in high school."

"All's fair in love and war," he says, repeating a line from the movie and what I had actually told Keatyn when we dated briefly in high school. Whitney had sent me a text—a simple text, *baby, please*—begging me not to go away with Keatyn for the weekend but stay with her and try and work out our relationship. She had devastated me when she had broken up with me a few months before and to have her now saying she made a mistake, was what I had longed to hear. I realized too late, that I was an idiot for not staying with Keatyn and tried to win her back. For a short period, she dated both Aiden and I.

"You wooed her. How did you know what to do? What would affect her?"

He shrugs. "I was just there for her when she was upset. I took her chocolate cake."

I think back to the movie. "And gave her a four-leaf clover for luck, put stars above her bed, ran a feather earring across her neck, and brought her dirt. None of those things really cost money."

"I bought her a purse she loved and some gorgeous gold feather earrings. But it's not what you spend that matters, Dawson. You have to find what touches her soul and give from yours freely."

"I was going to give her this." I show Aiden the

necklace I planned to give Vanessa tonight. "It's just something the girls and I found in Venice, but the butterfly stands for rebirth and the infinity symbol on its wings reminded me of our path back to each other."

"Why didn't you give it to her?"

"It felt insignificant after seeing all those jewels. Hard to compete with them."

Aiden smiles at me. "Here's a tip, Dawson. All *isn't* fair in love and war, but the victor always plays with heart."

IN THE CAR – L.A.
Riley

I'M ON MY way to the hotel to meet Shelby when I get a text.

> **Ariela:** *I'm really sorry the note upset you. That wasn't my intention.*

I don't reply, instead I call Logan. Once we exchange greetings, I get to the subject at hand.

"So tell me about this new guy she brought in to be her assistant."

"Kyle? I don't know much about him. Seems like a nice enough kid. Good looking. Funny. Maggie and Grandma were drooling over him."

"And what about Ariela?"

"They seem close. But they must not be too close because he thinks that Maggie and I are renewing our vows, so Ariela doesn't trust him enough to tell him everything."

"Is she fucking him?"

"Hmm, not sure. Based on the way he acts around her, I'd say he wants to but hasn't. Why the twenty questions? I thought after homecoming you two made up? She even told us about the premiere girl getting pregnant. I was under the impression she wasn't going to let that interfere with your relationship."

"Did she tell you guys about the note?"

"What note?"

"On graduation day, she was too chicken to tell me in person that she was going to Princeton."

"What do you mean? She told you in person then ran to her parents' car and left."

"Yeah, I know. But that wasn't her plan. Apparently, she didn't have the guts to tell me in person, so she was going to leave a note on my car. But as she was going to my car, she ran into me, blurted everything out, and forgot to give me the note. She's kept it all these years though. She gave it to me at homecoming and made me read it last night."

"And, what did it say?"

"That she had to go to Princeton because it was her dream, that she hoped I would understand, and that she hoped we could stay together."

"What the fuck?"

"That was my exact response."

"Why didn't she mail you the letter? Or message you? Or one of us? Anything?"

"Exactly. Why didn't she? If she was as heartbroken as she claims to have been, why didn't she send it?"

"Did you ever contact her after that?"

"Fuck no."

"Maybe that's why she didn't send it."

"It really doesn't matter anymore. We agreed to talk this week, but I'm bailing on that. At the wedding, I'll tell her I don't want to see her again, and she can go back home."

"Uh—"

"Uh, what?"

"She agreed to work for Asher, helping to design our new wedding and event space. She'll be around."

"Shit. I'm the one who encouraged her to take the job."

"Riley, maybe you should talk to her in person before you make a permanent decision. She's been working really hard. The wedding is going to be beautiful. Want to know what Maggie told me?"

"Probably not."

Of course, it doesn't stop him from saying, "Ariela told Maggie that she thinks making Keatyn's wedding perfection will prove her love to you."

"That makes no sense."

"Women never do," he says.

I PULL UP to the hotel and leave my car with the valet, our conversation replaying in my head and wondering what the hell I should do. It's hard to forgive someone who caused you so much pain—let alone let them back into your life.

My heart wants to go to the vineyard, hold Ariela in my arms, and have her tell me she still loves me.

I want her to keep telling me that until I believe

her.

Because after reading the note, I'm not sure I ever will again.

AS I KNOCK on the door to Shelby's bungalow, I focus on the task at hand. I'm here to take Shelby out for dinner, get to know her, and then fuck away any and all thoughts of Ariela.

When Shelby answers the door, my jaw drops to the floor.

"I look different, huh?" she purrs, handing me a glass of champagne. "I learned something today, Riley Johnson."

"What's that?"

"Do you remember the good champagne we had in New York?"

"Uh, yeah."

"I found out that it's actually a cheap brand. I think the sommelier steered you wrong."

"Oh, that sucks," I say, feeling bad for lying to her. "Um, you look amazing."

She does a little twirl, allowing me to check her out. Her hair has been changed from its usual bleached blond to a softer shade with brown undertones. Undertones are probably something a guy like me shouldn't know about, but I do. Keatyn always has very precise descriptions for the actresses she wants cast in our movies. Anyway, Shelby looks gorgeous, and I can't help but appreciate it. Her boobs are restrained in a low-cut gown that has sheer mesh covering her cleavage while still giving a hint of the creamy skin beneath. The rest of the black dress drapes fluidly over her curves, but isn't the skintight version she usually prefers. Her makeup is soft and pretty rather than harsh and dark. The effect is stunning, really.

"I've been totally pampered today," she says, reaching for my zipper. "I'd like to pamper you in return."

I grab her hand. "Although I would love to have your kind of pampering, you look too beautiful. Let's go to dinner first."

She freezes, staring at me with wide eyes. "Really, Riley? You think I look beautiful? Like not just hot, but actually *pretty?*"

"Yes, you look beautiful. And I told you, I want to get to know you better. Let's go eat then when we come back *I* will pamper you."

She grabs my face and kisses it then puts her arm in the crook of my elbow, allowing me to escort her out the door.

AT DINNER, I learn more about her family. And the picture is not pretty. She ran away at sixteen and has been on her own ever since. Her mom worked two jobs to make ends meet and she had a deadbeat stepfather. When Shelby started developing, he took notice. Although he hadn't done anything inappropriate yet, she says she knew it was coming. He'd snuck into her bedroom one night and told her what they were going to do. Fortunately, her mom got off early, and he didn't have the chance. She didn't stick around to find out if he was serious. She moved in with an older guy, and together they went to Vegas. She got a fake ID and worked underage as a dancer. After they broke up, she moved to L.A. with dreams of becoming an actress.

"You never told me you wanted to be an actress," I say, as the waiter refills my champagne and removes our dinner plates.

"Isn't that what every girl who comes here dreams of? Then reality sets in after you've gone to what feels like a million casting calls."

"You know, I could get you a part in a movie."

"You told me you don't cast girls who you sleep with."

"I never have before." She smiles a pretty, white-toothed smile. "Did you get your teeth whitened too?"

She laughs and covers her mouth with her hand. "Tyler made me."

"Tyler did good," I say again, reveling in her beauty. "I bet if you looked like this, you would have been cast long before I ever met you."

"I didn't really know how to look—or act—like a lady. I've been watching the women here. They behave differently. Their body language. The way they hold themselves, like they are all royalty even if they're not. You know, some of those Housewives were filming here today. It was exciting. I love watching that show. All their drama. It's such an escape from reality because their drama is nothing like real life. None of them know what it's like to not have money to cover their rent. They complain about being so tired, but all they did was work out, go to lunch, and talk behind each other's backs. I mean, I highly doubt any of them have ever worked a double shift before. Now, that's tired."

"I like that you're so down to earth."

"I'm ready to get down to earth with you, Riley.

Could we skip dessert and go back to the room?"

"Yes, we can," I say, summoning the waiter for the check and looking forward to what's to come.

WEDNESDAY, OCTOBER 15TH
CAPTIVE FILMS - SANTA MONICA
Dawson

I CALL VANESSA'S cell phone only to get sent straight to voicemail. She was supposed to have attended a marketing meeting this morning but didn't show. And that's unlike her.

I'm torn between wanting to know and not wanting to know what happened with Bam last night. But my concern gets the best of me, so I call her house phone.

Her butler, Bernard, answers.

"I'm sorry to bother you, but I just wanted to check on Vanessa. She isn't answering her cell and missed a business meeting at Captive this morning."

"She must have forgotten. She is out on the terrace having brunch with Mr. Martinez. Would you like to speak with her or shall I relay a message?"

"Uh, neither. Thanks. I'll call her later."

I put my head down on my desk, feeling defeated.

He spent the night with her.

That tells me everything I need to know.

A FEW HOURS later, she walks into my office. Her eyes are a little red, and she looks like she didn't sleep.

I can't bear to think about what she was doing with him that kept her up all night.

"You missed the meeting this morning," I state.

"I had some personal issues to deal with," she says back.

"Yeah, I figured." I slide a stack of papers toward her. "Here are the notes. We're meeting again next week. I'll have Tyler message you the time." I put my head down, pretending to study my computer in hopes that she will leave.

"Dawson," she says.

I look up. "Did you need something else?"

"Yes, I need you to talk to me."

"About what?"

"Seriously?"

"Vanessa, what am I supposed to say when your ex-husband shows up with roses and jewels, you introduce me as a co-worker, and miss our morning meeting because you were having *brunch on the terrace* with him?"

She sits down with a loud sigh.

"You know in the movie, how when Whitney sent you that message and told you what you longed to hear?"

"Yes."

"That's how I felt last night. Bam told me all the things I wish he would have said after I miscarried."

"So you're getting back together?"

"That's what he wants. His father is dying."

"I'm sorry. That must be difficult for him."

"It is. He will soon be at the helm of their family empire. He's scared, honestly. And he's grown up a lot in the last few months."

"Well, good for him," I say, forcing my lips together. Why is she making excuses for a guy who treated her like shit? But then again, maybe it wasn't always like that, and who am I to judge.

"Dawson, I love you—"

"You don't have to say it. I get it. He's back. It's what you wanted. You can go back to living in billionaire fairytale land."

"I don't want to do this here, Dawson. Can you come over tonight so we can talk?"

"No. Sorry. I understand. I wish you the best." I look down, trying to fight back my emotions.

"Have it your way," she says, walking out of my office. I hear the door shut as I place my fingertips on the bridge of my nose and close my eyes.

What am I going to tell the girls? That love doesn't always work out the way you planned? That sometimes money trumps love? Maybe I was wrong to come out here. Keatyn said that I would be getting some money from the sale of the stock. I'll take it and use the money to buy a home rather than uprooting my girls' lives.

Then I can go back to being what I was when I got here.

Broke.

And broken.

TRINITY MOVIE SET – STUDIO CITY

WHEN I GET back to my trailer after filming for most of the day, I'm surprised to find Vanessa waiting for me outside.

"I wasn't expecting you," I say to her. "What's up? Please tell me the doctor didn't confirm my pregnancy or anything."

"We'd totally sue if he did. I'm here to talk to you about when you want to announce your wedding. Once it actually takes place, we won't be able to keep a lid on it. I think we should have a press release prepared. Your agent, Cade Crawford, called me asking about this fundraiser. Did you not tell him?"

"I haven't told anyone, really. That was the point of it being a secret."

"I know, I'm just surprised you didn't tell *him*."

"Is he coming?"

"Of course."

"Then I don't need to. Now, why are you really here?"

She sits down with a sigh.

"I need someone to talk to."

"What about?"

"Dawson. Bam."

"Bam? What about him?"

"He showed up at my house last night. Dawson was there. I had just asked him to move in with me."

"Peyton told me about your redecorating project. I think it's a great idea. A good compromise. Um, I called Dawson the other day to see how things went with the girls' school visit. He told me about the playroom."

She frowns then nods. "I hadn't shown anyone until I showed him."

"He also told me something else," I say gently. "Vanessa, why didn't you tell me that you can't have more children?"

Tears fill her eyes. "Because I thought if I didn't say it, it wouldn't be true."

I squeeze her hand. "I'm really sorry."

"It's okay. I made a decision. Regardless of what happens with Dawson, I'm going to pursue having a baby. I never discussed it with the doctor. I don't know if I just can't get pregnant or if I can't carry a baby, but I'm going to find out. And if that won't work, I'll hire a surrogate or adopt."

"Really, that's so amazing, Vanessa. I'll help in any way I can. Even if it's just for emotional support, okay? You can always talk to me."

"Thank you. That means a lot."

"Now, tell me about Bam and Dawson. You asked him to move in, what did he say?"

"He said yes. We made love. He told me the girls decided to come here for school. We were going out to celebrate. Then Bam showed up with roses and a huge ruby."

"Does he want to get back together?"

"Yes. His father is dying. He's retiring from polo and will be taking over the family empire. His mother called me the other day and told me I should take him

115

back. I told her no. I didn't expect him to show up at my door."

"Did he forget the whole part about him cheating on you? And what about the model?"

"She dumped him for someone younger."

"Ha! Serves him right! What did Bam have to say about Dawson being there?"

"Yeah, that's where things went downhill. I introduced Dawson to Bam as someone I work with. He looked hurt when I said it. Then he left."

"Ouch. Why did you do that?"

"Because I didn't want to have to explain it to Bam. You know how he is. If he thought Dawson was his competition, it would just make him try harder to win me."

"And what do you want?"

"That's the million dollar question," she says.

"More like the billion dollar question," I say with a laugh.

"After Dawson left, Bam asked for a bottle of wine. The wine that he told me never to open."

"The one he wanted in the divorce so badly?"

"Yes, I wouldn't give it to him because I figured he'd waste it on the bimbo. Anyway, we opened it, drank it, he told me he's changed. That he still loves me. That he will be faithful. Then he got down on his knee and told me he's loved me since he learned how to love. Then he proposed. Had a huge diamond ring to seal the deal."

"Seal the deal? Did you say yes?!"

"He's still waiting for my reply to that question."

"Why?"

"Because, Keatyn, you don't know what it's like to have someone you love devastate you like that. You don't know what it's like to dream they will change their mind after they left you and come back and tell you what a mistake they made. And there's something that touches your heart when you finally hear those words."

"But you love Dawson."

"Will you please tell me about his wife?"

I shake my head. "It's not my place. That's something he needs to share with you if and when he's ready."

"Fine. Will you at least tell me about the first time she tried to commit suicide?"

"You saw how she outed me at winter formal in the movie, right?"

"Yeah."

"Well, in the movie, we said that she didn't come back after winter break, but in real life she did. She sat alone at the lunch table, and I should have gone to sit with her, but Brooklyn had been kidnapped, and I had other things to worry about. That night we heard sirens, and I was afraid Vincent had broken in. The school was put on lockdown. But it was because Whitney had tried to kill herself. Peyton found her, was pretty hysterical, and felt responsible. I went to the hospital with her. Whitney's mom was a total bitch. Still is, actually. She was sitting in the waiting room calling everyone she knew and moaning about how what had happened was affecting her! I yelled at her. Found out the man I thought was her father was really her stepfather. Peyton and I contacted her dad, and he came to see her. Her family was messed up. Supposedly, she was going to kill herself another time before but Dawson stopped her."

"How?"

"I don't think he even knows this, but he knew she was upset over his brother, and he told her he hoped they could be friends anyway. He gave her a hug, and she cried all over his shoulder. I guess that's when she decided not to do it. And what got her and Dawson started."

"It's going to be hard to compete with a dead wife. Even if she was imperfect in life, she won't be that way in death."

"That's true. But then again, life is messy—it's supposed to be that way."

"That's a Brooklyn quote. I'm sorry I was so mean to you about him in high school. He was a good man and a good friend"—she stops and laughs—"Oh gosh. I just did it too."

"Did what too?"

"In real life, I thought he could be hypocritical and selfish. But now that he's gone—"

"You forget that. B was what he was—highly driven. And in the drive to succeed, he didn't want a relationship or kids. He acted like all that mattered in life were the waves and chillness, but he enjoyed his money. I loved and adored him as a friend, but I'm very glad—"

"That you met Aiden."

"Yeah."

"You hit the jackpot with that one."

"Vanessa, you just kicked your jackpot out of your house."

"Bam? I don't want a man who's an asshole. Just because he has money he thinks . . ."

"I wasn't referring to Bam."

She stops and looks at me. "Dawson? You think Dawson is my jackpot?"

"What matters is what you think. Actually, that's not right. What matters is how you *feel*. How he makes you feel. Aiden and I seem perfect because we have this amazing connection. We appreciate each other and thank God for every day we have together. But it started with a spark. An instant deep-in-my-soul feeling. A feeling that I was exactly where I belonged when he held my hand."

"I felt like that once."

"You did?"

"Yeah," she says softly. "Can I ask you another question?"

"Of course."

"When Dawson came for your eighteenth birthday party, was he dating Whitney?"

"No."

"To your knowledge, has he ever cheated on anyone?"

"No. He's not like that. The Johnson boys are wild, but even Camden, the wildest brother of them all, isn't a cheater. Their parents are happily married and they value family and friendships. They understand what a good relationship should be."

"At your party, Dawson and I went back in Tommy's office to drink scotch. He was a gentleman, touched my back as he led me through the doorway. I felt like a school girl. We talked, and he kissed me. Best kiss of my life. Hands down. I always wondered."

"This conversation makes me think of B. Maybe fate is giving you a second chance. Maybe you and Dawson were supposed to get together then, but you chose different paths."

"And you think fate brought our paths back together?"

"Yes."

"I've kissed a lot of boys, but that kiss was memorable."

"Vanessa, one of the things I've always admired about you is your confidence and knowing what you desire and going for it."

"Having Bam cheat on me and losing the baby, made me lose my confidence."

"You didn't lose it. It's still in you. What you went through has just made you more compassionate. And compassion is *not* a weakness. When I came back from Europe and was confused about Brooklyn, you gave it to me straight. You told me he just wasn't into me. I'm going to return the favor. Vanessa, Dawson is into you. Don't let Bam or anything that may have happened in the past get in the way of what matters."

"What matters? I'm not sure I even know anymore."

"It's all that *ever* matters. Love. Why are you even hesitating? You love him. You asked him to move in with you. You adore his daughters."

"Yeah, you're right."

"And while you're at it, tell Bam to pound some sand up his ass, for me, when you send him back to his yacht."

She kisses my cheeks, laughing, as she leaves.

THURSDAY, OCTOBER 16TH
CAPTIVE FILMS – SANTA MONICA

Dawson

I'M IN A bad mood. I haven't spoken to Vanessa since yesterday morning. I know I was a dick to her, but whatever. She wants to be with Moneybags, I hope she's happy.

Actually, that's not true. I hope she's miserable with him.

"You have a really bitchy and demanding woman calling for you," Tyler says over the speaker in my office. "I've already told her you were busy twice, but I think she's going to keep calling until you talk to her."

"Who is it?"

"She says she's your mother-in-law. Do you have a moment to find out what's so important?"

"Sure, put her through." I take a deep breath, pick up the handset, and greet her. "Mrs. Clarke, how are you?"

"Not very well, actually. I just heard that you're thinking of moving my grandchildren to that wretched place."

"You mean Los Angeles?"

"Yes, the Land of Make Believe. I won't allow it."

"I'm afraid you don't really have a say in it, Mrs. Clarke. My job is here, and the girls are excited to go to their new school."

"And just what kind of school is it?"

"It's a private school very worthy of your grandchildren. You would approve."

"Were you going to consult me on this?"

"Um, no. I wasn't."

"When were you going to tell me?"

"As soon as it's official. They visited the school this week, and we've had our interview, but we've yet to get a final response as to their acceptance."

"Ava told me she's moving. That she's going to be allowed to wear makeup. What are you thinking? Do you want your daughter to end up on a pole?"

I try really hard not to sigh audibly. It will just get her going more. "No, I'm not. And it's just clear mascara and some lip gloss. Not a big deal."

"I'm going to fight the move."

"And how are you going to do that?"

"I'm going to sue for custody. I have rights as a grandparent."

"You threatened to do that after Whitney killed herself. You didn't do it then, and you aren't going to do it now. You don't want to have to deal with the girls on a daily basis, and you know it."

"That's not true. I only want what's best for them. There's no reason you can't get a job here."

"I like my job in L.A. and, honestly, I think the

change will be good for the girls. A fresh start for all of us."

"So they can forget about their mother?"

"They are never going to forget about their mother."

"I don't know why you can't just stay here."

"Because my job is here, and I need to support them. You know, since your son-in-law stole all of my money."

She ignores my jab. "I assume you will all be here for the fundraiser on Whitney's birthday?"

"The girls will not be coming to the fundraiser this year. It wasn't an appropriate event for children. All you did was parade them around."

"You want them to forget her!"

"No, I don't!"

"Well, you had better be here!"

"I'm going to try to attend, but I'm not making any promises."

"Try to attend? No. You will be in attendance along with my granddaughters, and that is final!"

"The girls will definitely not be attending. They will be starting their first week of school."

"Already? I assumed you would let them finish the semester!"

"I'm afraid not."

"This is asinine. I won't allow it. I expect the girls to finish the semester here, attend the fundraiser, and join the Clarke family for the holidays."

"Not gonna happen, sorry."

"Then you will be hearing from my attorney. I'm taking you to court."

"Oh, hey, speaking of court. I heard William had his sentencing."

"Yes, he got four years in prison."

"That's not nearly long enough, but I'm glad to know my testimony helped put him away."

"You shouldn't be so hard on him. He has a wife and three children."

"He stole all our money and your daughter killed herself because of it. You should hope he rots in jail like I do. And if you even think about suing me for custody, I will come to the fundraiser and tell all your friends the truth about why Whitney killed herself." I slam the phone down, hanging up on the bitch as my brother walks in my office.

"What's wrong?" he immediately asks. "Are the girls okay?"

"They're fine."

"You look upset."

"Mrs. Clarke just called. Threatened to sue me for custody."

"Will she?"

"I don't think so. She is upset because I'm moving the girls to this *wretched place* and is convinced Ava will end up dancing on a pole because I'm going to let her wear clear lip gloss."

Riley laughs out loud. "She's a piece of work, isn't she?"

"Yeah, she is. The Whitney Clarke Memorial Fundraiser is next week. She wanted the girls to go again this year."

"After last year, you said you wouldn't let them."

"I won't."

"So are you ready for the board meeting tomorrow?"

"I guess. It sounds like the investors are in for a bit of a shock."

"They will be surprised, but they'll be getting a really high return on their investments, so I highly doubt you will hear any complaints."

"So how did Ariela take the news about Shelby's pregnancy?"

"She took the news fine."

"So does that mean things are going well between the two of you?"

"Things are not going anywhere between us."

"Why not?"

"Get this. She had me read the note she was going to give me on graduation day. It basically said she was going to Princeton, and she hoped we could stay together."

"What?"

"Exactly. If she really felt that way, why didn't she let me know? It's bullshit, and I'm done with her."

"Riley, are you sure?"

"No, not really, but I'm moving on. With Shelby."

"Shelby? The baby mama? Why?"

"Hey, you're one to talk. You married Whitney."

"You're thinking of marrying her?!"

"I don't know, maybe. She's not what I expected."

"What did you expect?"

"Well, when we were at the premieres, she was maybe not the most classy date I've ever had, but I sent her to a personal shopper and to the spa and now she looks amazing. She seems to want to learn more. She didn't have the best upbringing, and she's really sweet. Not to mention she's a hellcat in the bedroom."

I rub my face and now understand why when I wanted to marry Whitney my family was so upset. They believed I should marry for love. "I know it sounds hypocritical of me, but you should marry for love, Riley."

"Do you regret marrying Whitney?"

"That's a difficult question to answer. If I wouldn't have married Whitney, we wouldn't have had Harlow."

"And she's an amazing little girl."

"Exactly."

"If you had a do-over, would you do the same thing? After all you went through?"

"I want to tell you I wouldn't. That I shouldn't have married her. That I should have thought of myself. That I should have married for love. And now that I know what that feels like—"

"With Vanessa?"

I nod. "I wish I would've married someone I really loved. I want that for you, Riley. For you to be married to the love of your life."

"I'm not so sure that's Ariela."

"Only you know who it is, Riley. I'm just saying, don't settle. Fight for her if you love her. It sounds like you got mad at Ariela over something that happened more than a decade ago. You're going to have to let all that go if you're ever going to be able to move forward with her."

"Sounds like the advice you should be giving yourself."

"What makes you say that?"

"I had a call with Vanessa earlier today. She said you won't talk to her."

"Did she tell you her ex spent the night?"

"In the guest house. You have no idea how much he hurt her. There's no way she'd ever take him back."

"You didn't see the ruby he gave her."

"He also proposed."

"He *what*? What did she say?"

Riley smirks at me. "She hasn't given him an answer yet. Sounds like you need to take your own advice, bro, and fight for what *you* want."

SHELBY'S BUNGALOW – SUNSET BLVD.

AFTER A MORNING prenatal massage, a blowout and makeup application, and a lovely poolside lunch, I have the hotel driver take me to the sports bar where Marcy works. I purposely dressed in my old clothes so I wouldn't stand out. If I came in all classy, the people I'm friends with who work here would ask questions. Dressed like this, me sitting at the bar while Marcy works is a normal occurrence. There are two customers eyeing me from the end of the bar. Businessmen, in town for one of the conferences held at the hotel up the street, most likely. I'm wearing a pair of skintight jeans, cheap black booties, and a white T-shirt that shows off the cleavage God blessed me with.

Really, the cleavage is what they are staring at.

Bleach-blonde Shelby would have flirted with them.

The new Shelby will not.

I ignore them and sit down in front of Marcy, who is filling glasses from the tap.

"Hey," she says, sliding one of the beers in front of me. "What's up? You decide to slum or is the gig up, and you need a place to stay?"

"I have something for you." I smile at her and hand her an envelope. She sets it on the wet counter, delivers beer to the men, and then comes back.

"It's not even my birthday," she says, ripping the envelope open. When she sees the check, her eyes widen. "Is this a joke?"

"No, I've had incredible fortune lately and am living my dream, and I want that for you too. I didn't have much of a family and being able to send you back to yours would mean a lot to me."

She runs out from behind the bar and throws her arms around me in an uncustomary show of emotion.

"Oh my God! I'm so excited! My parents will be so happy!"

"And you can do what you love."

She jumps up and down.

"Is this for real? Will the check bounce?"

"No, it won't," I say, holding up my hand to discreetly show off a very large, but very fake engagement ring.

"What is that?" she asks, pulling my hand into the light. "It's so big it almost doesn't look real."

"I know. It's crazy. The bigger they are, the faker they look. But, trust me, it's real. We're getting married!"

"Really? God, you work fast, girl. When is it? I want to come!"

"Oh, I so wish you could," I lie. "But we're going to the Maldives. Just the two of us." I quickly change the subject. "So when will you leave for home?"

"As fast as I can pack my shit up and go. Thank you, Shelby. You're an amazing friend."

"You're welcome, and don't be a stranger. Text me with lots of updates!"

"I absolutely will," she says sincerely.

THE SECOND I leave the bar, I drop my phone on the concrete, causing the glass to shatter.

I carefully pick it up and call Tyler.

"I'm so klutzy. I dropped my phone, and it broke."

"I'll order you a new one," he says.

"Do you think you could get me a new number? Mine is one digit off a pizza place, and I get *so* many wrong numbers."

"Sure thing. Anything else you need?"

"No, but I didn't get a chance to thank you for setting me up with the personal shopper. She was really nice."

"It was my pleasure," he says, then ends the call.

I get in the town car, pour myself a glass of complimentary champagne, roll down the window, and chuck the fake ring out.

Then I lean back into the plush seat.

The only person who knows the baby isn't Riley's is gone.

Now, I just need to figure out how to manipulate a

paternity test.

And get him to put a ring on it for real.

KEATYN & AIDEN'S HOME – MALIBU
Keatyn

"THAT WAS SOME birthday party," Aiden says as we're getting in the car to head home.

"I feel like I didn't really get to spend much time with the girls but, then again, this party was more for their friends."

"And apparently they have a whole lot of them. The place was packed," Aiden says.

"Well, that's to be expected. All three girls have such different interests, so you had guests from the music, fashion, and movie industries. Tommy and Mom went a little crazy on their gifts, but it's their eighteenth birthday, of course they'd do it up big."

"Most of the night, I was reminiscing about your eighteenth birthday party. Remember how we danced all night long?"

"I wish we could have danced more tonight."

"Why didn't you want to?"

"I'm tired, for one, but I also felt kinda old."

"You're not old."

"I know, it's just that in my head I still feel like I'm eighteen, but when you are at a party with people that age, you realize you're not really as young as you think."

Aiden wraps his arm around my shoulder and gives

me a squeeze. "I'm glad we aren't that young. I much prefer our life now to our life then."

"You do?"

"Yes, I do." He tilts his head slightly. "I take that back. We did have a lot of fun. It's just that I'm really looking forward to what's next for us—a slower pace, spending more time together, and raising a family."

"I'm excited too. Did you notice Gracie was dancing with that Dylan kid?"

"He's in that boy band, right? Isn't that how you said she got to Eastbrooke's homecoming? She hitched a ride on their plane?"

"Yeah, which was kind of weird. At homecoming, she seemed all into Baylor Hawthorne."

"I know his dad. He's a good kid. But you remember what it's like to be that age. You like a different person every week."

"That's true, I guess."

"The boy band guy seems a little old for her though."

"He's seventeen."

"And she's fourteen."

"She'll be fifteen in a few weeks."

"I know, but I just didn't like where his hands were. I'm surprised Tommy allowed it. I'm not even her dad, and I was ready to go kick his ass."

"That's pretty sweet of you," I tell him. "What are you going to do when it's your daughter out there?"

"I'll definitely be kicking some ass. No way is some little punk going to get away with that shit."

"You danced like that with me when *we* were in high school," I tease.

He waves his hand, like *whatever.* He's so cute, and I am dying to tell him about the triplets, but now doesn't feel like the right time. When I tell him, I want it to be special, not when we're both exhausted after a long day.

"You still haven't told me where we're going on our honeymoon," I pout. "How am I supposed to know what to pack?"

"You're going to be naked the entire time. No need for clothes," he says, sounding serious.

"Come on, Aiden. Give me a hint. Or at least a rough idea of the climate so I can pack."

"You don't have to worry about that, actually. Kym is already at the vineyard, and she's packing for you."

"Can't I at least have a hint?"

He kisses me, which still fills my head with cotton candy, making me forget my question and focus solely on the feel of his lips on mine.

WHEN WE GET home, a little ball of fur races toward us, barking.

"This dog is a—how you say it—hell raiser?" Marvel says in greeting.

"What did she do now?" Aiden says, laughing, while I cuddle with our new puppy. I still can't believe Aiden surprised me with her the other night.

"She shredded one of my dishtowels, but then she fell asleep on my lap, and I can't be angry further. On that note, I bid you bonne nuit."

The puppy is on our heels as we head into our bedroom suite.

"We need to decide on a name for her," Aiden says

as we're getting ready for bed.

"I thought you had a list of possible names."

"I do. I've narrowed it down to three and want you to choose."

"Okay," I say, snuggling next to him in bed, the dog in between us, licking our faces with its rough little tongue.

"One I was thinking of is Chardonnay, since she'll be at the vineyard, and she's yellow."

"That's cute."

"Another idea is Grigio, same reasons."

"Hmm. I don't really like that one. What else have you got?"

"Bliss."

"Oh, Aiden," I say, my eyes filling with tears. "Do you remember?"

"*Vos lèvres sont mon béatitude.* Of course, I remember telling you that your lips are my bliss, Boots." He kisses me. "Especially because they still are."

"I love the name. It's perfect for her." I rub the puppy's ears. "What do you think, *Bliss?*"

The puppy lays her head on Aiden's chest, sighs, and closes her eyes.

"She's in love with you, just like I am," I tell Aiden, lying my head on his shoulder, sighing, and feeling pretty blissful myself. "When I went to my doctor's appointment, he told me the date when we probably conceived. Remember the day we were up at the vineyard, and we took the Gator out, got caught in the rain, and ended up covered in mud?"

"I remember you kissing me and telling me it reminded you of when we got caught in the rain that

133

night at the Cave in high school."

"That was one of the best kisses of my entire life," I confess. "So was the one in the mud, apparently."

"You think that's when we got pregnant?"

"It had to be. You'd been traveling, and I'd been filming. Remember, we met up there for the weekend?"

"I do remember," he says, gently caressing my face. "I also remember you laughing, stripping off my clothes, and telling me I was a filthy boy."

"Things got dirtier after that," I laugh. "I just thought that was kind of fun. It was spur of the moment. One of the best kisses of my life followed by one of the best sexual experiences of my life—that resulted in us being pregnant."

He picks the puppy up off his chest and gently puts her in her kennel. When he gets back in bed, he pulls me close and gives me another one of his amazing kisses.

Which definitely leads to something more.

SHELBY'S BUNGALOW – SUNSET BLVD.

Shelby

RILEY WALKS INTO my bungalow—doesn't that just sound so cool, *my bungalow*—and I'm waiting with drink in hand. He's been coming over every night, and even though he says he doesn't do commitment, he sure seems committed to learning more about me.

Although, we've done more fucking than talking,

he did take me to a charity event last night. Which I thought was a positive step. And I looked totally ah-mazing in one of the evening gowns I bought this week. Okay, so technically I didn't buy it. And I'm going to have to figure out something quick. Although I have a very nice roof over my head and all the spa, food, and drinks I could want, I'm going to need some money, and I haven't worked in a while.

Not to mention, my boss is threatening to fire me if I don't work this weekend. But I'll be honest, I'd rather stay here than work.

Riley takes his suit jacket off and makes himself at home.

"I ordered us a romantic dinner to be served here," I tell him. "Thought we could stay in tonight."

"That sounds good," he says, pulling off his tie. "It's been a busy day. What did you do?"

"I had a doctor's appointment," I lie.

"What did he say? Everything progressing well?"

Oh, yes, I think, things are progressing perfectly—except for one minor detail.

"He said my blood pressure was a bit high and suggested I stay off my feet. I'm back on the schedule at work next week, and I'm not sure what I'm going to do."

"How much do you make there, including tips?"

I give him a number that is about double what I really make.

"Wow, that's not bad," he whistles.

I prance over next to him, letting him get an eyeful of my chest. "What can I say? Guys like to look, and as long as I don't mind and bring them their drinks, they tip well."

"If the doctor wants you off your feet, you need to listen to him. Why don't you look for a job doing something where you can sit?"

"No one is going to hire someone who is pregnant, Riley."

"You can't even tell you're pregnant."

"I'll be showing soon enough."

"Tell you what. I'll give you an allowance of what you usually make while you look for a job. How's that sound?"

"Oh, Riley! You are so wonderful!" I allow myself to fall across his lap and then kiss his neck.

Unfortunately, the doorbell rings.

I give his crotch a squeeze as I get up. "Maybe we should skip dinner and go straight to dessert."

He chases after me, slapping my ass. "Why don't I let room service in while you go get naked?"

"Sounds like a plan."

I go into the bedroom and strip down, deciding to put on one of the new pieces of lingerie I bought. This gown is a gorgeous silk and lace chemise, and it's very different from my usual sex-store stuff.

But it still shows off my body. My boobs are spilling out over the front, and my ass is showcased by the short hemline.

Riley will love it. Especially once he sees what I ordered for *dinner*.

"This is an interesting meal," he says, carrying the tray of chocolate covered strawberries, chocolate sauce, and freshly made whipped cream into the bedroom. "You're not naked."

"What do you think of what I'm wearing?"

He brushes his hand across the silk. "It's too pretty to get covered in chocolate. Take it off." I do as he asks. I love when he's bossy and commanding. "Undress me, then cover me with something on this tray, and eat it off."

I strip off the lingerie and am unzipping his pants when his phone rings.

He looks at the number, says, "I need to take this," and steps out of the room.

I carefully open the door just a bit so I can eavesdrop. And based on the gentle tone of his voice, I know he's talking to *her*.

And we can't have that.

SHELBY'S BUNGALOW – SUNSET BLVD.

Riley

"RILEY, WE WERE supposed to talk this week," Ariela says to me when I take the call. "I know you were upset over the note, but at Eastbrooke we promised to put the past behind us and focus on our future. On if we have a future."

"I wanted that, but now I'm not sure about all this. I can't begin to understand why you did what you did to me."

"I can't understand why you never contacted me either. You act like you're the only one who got hurt. I knew I was going to hurt you, Riley, but I never imagined you'd completely give up on us."

"I can't deal with this right now. We'll talk this weekend," I say then hang up.

JUST AS I end the call, the doorbell rings again. I answer it to find room service with a full-blown steak dinner.

"Hey, Shelby, get dressed. Let's eat. I'm starving."

She comes out—naked this time—and sits down at the table. "Did I hear you saying something about this weekend?"

"Yeah, I have an out-of-town event to attend."

"Oh, how fun! What should I pack? Do I need to get anything new?"

Part of me wants to take her to the wedding so that I can show Ariela I don't need her.

I really don't understand my desire to hurt Ariela when all I've ever wanted to do is love her. But if I take Shelby, I'm pretty sure we'd never get back together. I'd be putting the final nail in our love coffin.

And I'm not ready to do that.

"No, it's a small private event. Friends and family only."

"Where is it?"

"Northern California. Wine country."

"Keatyn and Aiden have a winery up there. Is that where you're going?"

"No," I lie. "It's just a fundraiser."

"A fundraiser for friends and family only? That sounds more like a wedding. Surely, you can bring a guest."

"I'm going to be busy and wouldn't be able to entertain you."

"I can entertain myself. It would be good to get away."

"Except the doctor suggested you stay off your feet. You'd be on your feet at this event, so it's probably best for you and the baby to stay put."

"But—" she presses. "Maybe I'll stowaway in your suitcase."

"Look, Shelby, I've been here every night trying to get to know you better."

"I'll say. Last night you got to know my ass pretty up close and personal."

I stop eating and put my fork down. "You're right. I did. Is that not something you'd like to continue?"

"What? No. I love sex with you, Riley. I never know what to expect." She gives me a very intimate and sexy look. The kind that should cause my dick to salute her. Except that what Ariela said to me keeps running through my head. "It sounds like you're confusing my wanting to get to know you on a personal level with getting to know you on a sexual level. No offense to you, but I don't have a problem finding women to sleep with. So maybe we should take sex out of the equation so as not to further complicate our already complicated situation."

She doesn't reply.

I look at my watch. Knox texted me earlier and told me to meet him at the club. He exaggerated and said we haven't been out in forever. I told him I'd see him all weekend, but he said it's hardly the same thing.

I finish off the rest of my meal and set my napkin down.

"Thanks for dinner," I tell her, like she had some-

139

thing to do with its preparation and trying not to think about what's still waiting for us in the bedroom. After talking to Ariela, my dick probably wouldn't cooperate anyway. It seems to have a crush. "I've got to get going."

"What? But, daddy," she pouts. "We haven't had dessert yet."

"Sorry, I'll have to take a rain check on that." I kiss her cheek. "Take it easy, stay off your feet, and have a good weekend. I'll call you when I get back in town."

She tries to kiss me on the lips, but I move too fast and manage to escape.

I LOOK DOWN at my phone and see that Ariela sent me a text. Just seeing her name pop up on the screen makes my heart hurt. Maybe my brother is right.

> **Ariela:** *You hung up on me. Please don't do that. I'm calling you back. Will you answer and talk to me, please?"*

I call her back instead.

"We don't have to decide at the wedding, Riley," she says softly. God, I love the sound of her voice. "Once it's over, I can come back to L.A. if you want to hang out. Don't laugh, but do you remember the date that never ended in the music video we shot and how we recreated it that day? All the fun stuff we did? I want to do it again."

My heart sinks into my stomach as I remember how beautiful she looked. I can still picture her little blue dress fluttering around her legs as she ran through waves. "We made love under the pier that night."

"That was one of the best parts of the date. And it's okay if you can't do it, but I'm going to. I want to revisit all those magical places."

"Once the wedding is over, I'm taking a few days off myself. I'd like to go with you, Ariela. But that's all I can promise."

"That's all I'm asking for. See you tomorrow."

"See you tomorrow," I say, my heart practically singing with joy at the thought.

As soon as I hang up, I get another text from Knox.

Knox: *We're waiting.*

Me: *Who's we?*

Knox: *Me and your brother. He's drunk and broken-hearted. It's a horrible combination for picking up women. I can see why you didn't want to hang out with me after the makeup bitch. Please send help.*

When I get to the club, I find them in the VIP section, as expected.

Knox points toward Dawson, who's staring at his phone. "Miss Bossy Pants."

"He's in love with her," I state.

"Yeah, but he's either too fucking stubborn or too fucking stupid to do something about it. Apparently, that trait runs in the family. I heard you've been shacking up with Shelby."

"I'm not shacking up with her."

"You've been with her every night since Ariela let you read the stupid note."

"How do you even know about that?"

"Keatyn and I work together every day. Between her and Tyler, they know everything."

I roll my eyes.

"So I brought you here to give you some advice." He hands me a shot of tequila. "Stop playing hide the salami with the baby mama. And before you go on about the note, I'm going to tell you that you're behaving like a fucking idiot. And if Ariela is still single at the wedding, she's free game, and Knox will be on the hunt."

My blood starts to boil just like it did that night at dinner when I broke my hand. I look down at the splint still on it, reliving the pain I felt when I punched the tree along with the spot-on thing Grandpa Douglas asked. *What hurts worse, Hollywood? Your hand or your heart?*

Since Ariela has come back into my life, my heart has hurt worse than ever before.

"I don't know what to do."

"And fucking Shelby is the path of least resistance?"

I nod.

"Is that what you want out of life, Riley? I just bought a fucking house on the hill. I'm building a studio with Keatyn. I'm going to settle down. I think it's time we both do. I mean, look at all these girls," he continues, pointing out to the dance floor. "It's not like going home to the same woman every night. Although I know that the makeup girl was a bitch, and I'm glad to be rid of her, I do miss coming home to someone. We have everything, Riley. It's time we let ourselves share it. Now, go take your drunk brother home before I throw him to the wolves."

I look at Dawson and sigh. It's hard to give advice to someone when you won't take it yourself.

FRIDAY, OCTOBER 17TH
CAPTIVE FILMS - SANTA MONICA
Riley

"ARE YOU READY for this?" Keatyn asks me, as we make our way into the boardroom. "It's weird, really. You'll be announced as chairman and then your first order of business will be the sale of the company. Are you sure we're doing the right thing?"

I put my arm around her and give her a squeeze. "You know we are."

"It's hard though. To work so hard and then give it all up."

"We aren't giving it up, Keatyn," Dallas says. "We're cashing out. We should be celebrating."

"We will be tonight," I say, trying to help her focus on the positive.

AFTER A SUCCESSFUL meeting, we get all the employees together to tell them the news. Dallas hands out fake checks that show them how much their stock options will be worth when the deal closes.

143

It's safe to say based on the screams of joy, the tears, and the grateful hugs, that they're for the sale.

And their celebration seems to ease Keatyn's mind.

"THAT WENT BETTER than I expected," she says, as we get settled on the plane to Sonoma, along with Knox, Grandpa Douglas, Dawson, and Vanessa.

"So are you excited for the wedding?" Vanessa asks Keatyn.

"Yes, I just hope it all turns out the way I imagined it would. I didn't give Ariela much time to pull it together, so I'm going to try not to stress."

"Well, my job as your maid of honor is to make sure you have a stress-free wedding. Kym said we'll have a busy morning tomorrow trying on dresses."

"We will. I can't believe I'm getting married in twenty-four hours and still don't know what I'm wearing. But Kym always comes through."

"When is the family coming up?"

"Not until tomorrow. On Sunday, before we leave for our honeymoon, we'll do our typical family birthday celebration for the girls. Anymore, it's so hard to get us all in one place. Ivery leaves Sunday night for a concert in Spain, and Emery has a shoot in New York."

"I heard you took over publicity for Ashlyn Roberts," Knox says to Vanessa. "When are you going to work with me?"

"Whenever you ask."

"I'd like you to do the publicity for me and Keatyn's new project. She slipped it to the press the other night, so I figure we should drop a more few more hints while the time is right."

"I can do that," Vanessa says.

I notice that Dawson and Vanessa aren't sitting beside each other. Actually, I don't think they've even spoken to each other since we left the office.

He looks miserable and I'm pretty sure it has nothing to do with his hangover.

"You working?" I ask, sitting down next to him.

"Yeah, just going through emails. With the sale, everyone has a lot of questions."

"What do they want to know?"

"Mostly, what's next for the three of you."

"And have you told them?"

"Not yet. But I at least wanted to reply."

I lower my voice. "Based on the way you're ignoring Vanessa, I'm assuming you didn't take my advice."

"No, I didn't. I think it's best that we go our separate ways."

"Why? She makes you fucking happy."

"Speaking of fucking. If you love Ariela—which I know you do—why are you still fucking Shelby?"

I shake my head. "Fuck if I know."

"I do know, actually," he tells me. "Because it's easier to do that than risk your heart again."

The pilot lets us know we're cleared for takeoff, so I go back to my seat next to Keatyn. Although I'd like to help my brother, all he's going to do is turn it around on me. And I don't need to deal with that right now.

We need to be celebrating.

Besides, we'll be in Sonoma soon enough.

"WHATCHA READING?" I ask Keatyn, who is studying something on her phone.

She rolls her eyes and shows me an article.

The Triplets are Legal. The Triplets are Legal.

As if there are any men reading this who don't already know.

But for those of you ladies who have been wondering why your man has been glued to the internet this morning, it's because the world's most beautiful triplets, Avery, Emery, and Ivery Stevens, daughters of Tommy Stevens and Abby Johnston, officially turned eighteen today.

Last night they celebrated in style with a swanky party attended by their celebrity friends, and those little minxes blessed their followers with numerous live party videos.

This trio is used to being in the spotlight. Not only do they have famous parents, but they are making names for themselves.

Avery has been juggling interning in the marketing department at Captive Films with designing clothes for the successful Stevens clothing brand. Emery has been gracing catwalks around the world, and Ivery is home for a short time before continuing her European music tour.

Now for the party details:

— The girls made a big entrance, arriving in a pink helicopter decked out in tight club clothes and sky-high designer shoes.

—Little sister, Gracelyn, danced all night with none other than the youngest Summer Boy crooner, Dylan, who posted a photo of the two of them kissing, causing thousands of teeny bopper

hearts around the world to break.

— Twenty-four-year-old bad boy rapper, Treska, who has been romantically linked to Emery even though they say they are just friends, didn't try to hide their relationship last night. The pair are clearly a couple who were just waiting for her birthday to make it official.

— Ivery spent the evening surrounded by her girl power posse, who posted most of the sexy pics and videos that set the male population a flutter.

— The on and off again couple, Keatyn Douglas and Knox Daniels, showed up fashionably late together after attending a Trinity wrap party with the local crew.

—And what did Daddy Stevens buy his now legal daughters? A trio of the megahot red "Rosso Bia" Lamborghini Aventador Superveloce. (Which for those of you who don't speak Italian means, super fast and super expensive—to the tune of about a half million dollars apiece—along with a brand new Gulfstream jet for them to share.

P.S. Can I just say that Tommy is one of those men who keeps getting sexier the older he gets. That little splash of grey at the temples. Meow. I'd totally go reverse cougar all over him.

P.P.S. Speaking of that, I need to know how Abby Johnston always looks like she's found the fountain of youth. Dealing with four high profile and successful teenaged daughters ought to give anyone a few wrinkles, but Abby seems to take it all in stride. Or else she's got a really good plastic surgeon.

"What upsets you about that? They wrote a similar article after your eighteenth."

"Although I should be happy no one knows about the wedding and thinks Knox and I are together, I hate when they talk about me and Knox as a couple."

"But for years, the two of you haven't set the record straight because it was good for business."

"I know. It's hard sometimes, though."

I grab her hand. "Just think, tomorrow you are marrying the love of your life. And that's all that matters."

She gives my hand a squeeze. "You're right. That's all that's ever mattered."

ASHER VINEYARDS – SONOMA COUNTY

VANESSA IS IN the kitchen helping Keatyn prepare a cheese tray for everyone to snack on. I don't know what to do about her. I really don't.

But I do know that I love her.

I should be a man. Talk to her.

But I don't know what to say. Don't know if she even wants to talk to me.

She looks up from what she's doing and smiles in my direction. It's a soft, sad smile.

And it wrecks me.

I catch her eye, nod my head in the direction of the room I'm staying in, and head that way—praying like hell she will follow.

When I open the door and turn around, I'm happy to find her standing alongside me. I smile and allow her to go in first.

She perches on the edge of the bed. "Hey," she says.

"Hey," I say back.

"Are you still mad at me?"

"I'm not sure what I am," I answer honestly.

"Dawson, will you let me explain about Bam? Like actually listen and try to understand?"

I nod.

"When we split, it devastated me. I couldn't eat. Couldn't sleep. Couldn't work. I could barely get out of bed. Losing the baby and being told I couldn't have more children broke me. To make matters worse, my husband was with another woman when it happened. He didn't support me. Even though when it happened I swore I never wanted to see him again, there was a part of me that still loved him. That wanted him to come home, take me in his arms, and tell me it would be okay."

"Which he finally did this week."

"Two years too late. I'm sorry that I introduced you as my coworker and not my love. But you don't know Bam. He's used to getting what he wants. If he thought I was with someone else, it would only make him want me more."

I squint my eyes. "You don't want to make him want you more?"

149

"No, I don't. I'm glad that we got a divorce, and I have no desire to get back together with him."

"I heard he proposed."

"He did. And we had the most heartfelt conversation we've had in years. It was something that I needed."

"Why?"

"So I could get some closure and truly move on. With you, I hope. I still want you and the girls to move in with me."

"Vanessa, I love you, but I don't think I'm the right guy for you. So, I think it's best that we both cut our losses and move on."

"Dawson, what aren't you telling me? I know that you're keeping something from me. You made me get naked, but I don't think you have."

"You don't get it. I don't want to talk about it. I don't want to keep dredging up the past. I'm trying to get over it! I've been trying for two years to get over it!" I yell.

"You're upset just talking about talking about it. I need to know, Dawson. I need to understand."

"Fine. You want the truth, here it is. Everything I have—the house, the car, the suits, the credit cards—isn't mine. I'm broke. No retirement. No savings. Nothing. I couldn't have moved here if it weren't for Keatyn's generosity. I couldn't have even gotten a cheap apartment. I have no money. You have everything. And whatever you don't have, Bam wants to give you." Fuck. I can't do this. "Not only can I not give you anything, you don't fucking need anything. I have nothing to offer you."

"Why don't you have any money, Dawson?"

I shake my head.

"You made me get naked and tell you everything. What haven't you told me? What did you do?"

"What did *I* do? Oh sure, it's my fault. That's exactly what everyone thinks. How did he not know? Easy. One day it was all there. The next day it was all gone. And within a few weeks, so was the guy she invested all our money with." I bury my face in my hands. "And then she was dead. She fucking killed herself because she lost all our money and was afraid to tell me. Afraid to tell me she hadn't made a house payment in months. That creditors were calling every day. She told me she made a bad investment, and we took a hit, but she said it would be fine. She lied." I look up at her. "Just go, Vanessa. Please. I have nothing to offer you."

ASHER VINEYARDS – SONOMA COUNTY

WE'RE SITTING ON the front porch of Aiden and Keatyn's house, rocking and chatting like we always do when we're here. Ariela is still hard at work but told me she'd meet up with me later.

"You know, I'm starting to think I'd like a place up in Sonoma," I say. "A place to get away. A place to raise a family. I'd like to have a place like our house in the Hamptons. Big enough where my whole family could stay, just on the opposite coast."

"I think your family would love that," Keatyn says.

"Do you think I could find something like that, close to you like Knox will be?"

"Knox's place is a stone's throw away," Grandpa says.

"I can have Aiden get you in touch with a local realtor," Keatyn tells me. "He always calls when land goes on the market, and a lot of times he calls before it does. You might also think about building what you want."

"Building? How long would that take?"

"At least a year, if not two—wait. There's a house that we went to a few years ago. The architecture was amazing. Very modern."

"I'm not sure if I like modern anymore."

"Riley, it's not the decor of your penthouse that feels cold, it's you being lonely. And even though this house is modern, it's got a ton of wood that makes it feel cozy."

Aiden, Dallas, and Knox join us on the porch.

"We wore Bliss out," Knox says. "Now, I want a dog. Have you ever seen such a little cutie?"

"Aiden," Keatyn says, "do you remember that house near here—the one I said was like a modern loft?"

"The Martins, Bud and Trish's house?"

"Yes, that's it. Do you think they would be interested in selling?"

"Well, I think with the right price they might. Their daughter moved to North Carolina, and they've been saying they miss their grandkids. You want me to call them?"

Keatyn raises an eyebrow in my direction. I shrug back. "Why not?"

"I mean, it can't hurt to ask," Keatyn encourages.

Aiden gets on the phone and makes a call while we all listen. The further along the conversation goes, the bigger her grin gets.

And I'll admit, mine does too. The couple seems amiable to an offer, so Aiden sets up a time for me to see the house tomorrow.

"I'll go with you," Knox tells me. "I close on my place in a couple weeks. I'm practically an expert."

"Keatyn, will you come inside with me?" Aiden says. "I can't find those crackers, and Marvel is down in the barn cooking up a storm."

"Uh, sure," she says.

"Bring some more wine out when you come," I tell her as they go inside.

"Where's your brother and Miss Bossy Pants?" Knox asks.

"Miss Bossy Pants?" Grandpa says. "You must be referring to Vanessa."

"I am. She's something, huh?"

"She's smart. Speaking of smart, Hollywood. That Ariela that has your panties in a twist is also one smart cookie. If she were as confident in her personal life as she is in her professional one, she'd have you wrapped up in ribbons with flowers in your hair. Wait until you see this place tomorrow. I know most men aren't much for noticing the little shit, but that girl has got the details covered."

"Sounds like you have a crush," Grandma teases.

"If I was a single young man and hadn't already met the love of my life, I'd be on that like white on rice," Grandpa says with a laugh. "Speaking of that, Hollywood, you looked rode hard and hung up wet this morning. I heard you got some girl knocked up."

"We're not sure the baby is his," Dallas states.

"And if it is?"

"I'll take care of it," I assure him.

"Good man," he says. "Now, run on in the house and see what's taking them so long with the wine. It's colder than a witch's tit out here, and I need something to warm these old bones."

I'M THANKFUL FOR a reason to stop talking about Shelby and the baby. It's the last thing I want to be discussing when Ariela joins us. As I enter the kitchen, I notice movement out of the corner of my eye and see Aiden has Keatyn pushed into the corner of the pantry. His hand is up under her dress and they are kissing passionately.

And I know what's about to happen next.

I quickly vacate the kitchen and head back to the porch.

When I sit back down, Knox says, "Where's the wine?"

"Aiden is bringing it out. He'll be just a minute."

LATER IN THE evening, I pull Aiden aside.

"I gotta know. Did you just have a quickie in the pantry?" The immediate grin on his face tells me all I need to know. "Why?"

"Why what?"

"Why a quickie? You've been together forever. Don't you just do it missionary position in bed once a month by now?"

Aiden laughs and shakes his head. He's never been one to kiss and tell, but he says, "Not even close."

"I'm not trying to pry, and I don't want details, but I need to know how monogamy works. Tell me the last five times you did it and where."

"Well, the pantry about an hour ago. With her pregnancy, she's been really tired at night. And in the mornings, she's felt sort of sick."

"Oh, I get it. Had it been a while?"

He shakes his head again. "No. Okay, fine. Last five times were the quickie in the pantry, at three o'clock this morning—she woke up, couldn't go back to sleep, so she drug me outside and sat me in the chaise. She was on top the first time. I took her back to bed, and we finally got back to sleep around five—"

"Okay, so now you're just bragging."

He grins. "I'm lucky. But so is Dallas. He says baby number five happened when they did it in the back of a limo. Your sex life is what you make it, Riley. If you make your woman feel desired and loved, you'll never be bored in the bedroom." He grins. "Or, wherever."

"So all those times I think you're old and boring when you say you're tired and want to go home—"

"It's usually because we're horny."

"Jeez, why don't you just say that then?"

He doesn't reply, just lifts an eyebrow at me and walks out the door.

ASHER VINEYARDS – SONOMA COUNTY
Vanessa

DAWSON'S HEAD IS down. He's so upset.

I move behind him and give him a tight hug.

"I'm not leaving. I'm not leaving you, Dawson." I start crying. The thought of not being with him tears me to pieces. Back to the pieces of what was left after Bam. Dawson has made my heart whole again, and he doesn't even understand how valuable that makes him.

He keeps his head down and repeats, "I have nothing to give."

"Dawson, that's what you don't understand. You've already given me the one thing I've never truly had. The one thing I need. And that's love. In case you've never heard the saying *Money can't buy love*, it's true. I'm proof. I'll give it all away if you want. If it will put us on a level playing field. I just want love. I just want to be loved."

He raises his head slightly.

"I do love you."

"I know you do. I swear to you. It's all I'll ever need. Please."

He touches my face and pulls me onto his lap, kissing me and sliding his hands up my blouse.

"No," I say.

"Why?"

"Because you still haven't told me everything."

He hangs his head. "You're right. I haven't."

"The girls told me the other night that their mama spent all your money. How did she wipe you out? What did she do with the money?" I run my hand gently across my forearm.

"I really don't want to talk about it, Vanessa."

"You have to. I can see it in your eyes, Dawson. You need to. And I need to understand. Please tell me."

He takes a deep breath. "She always had issues with her family. Her sister, Winnie, was her mother's favorite and could do no wrong. Even though I told her over and over that what her family thought didn't matter, she was always trying to impress them. To get back in her mother's good graces. I traveled a lot for my job. We had a nanny that helped her take care of the kids, but because I worked a lot, a lot of the household duties were left to her, like paying the bills. Anyway, she invested all our money into some fund her mom told her about. It was Winnie's husband's deal, and she was trying to help.

"She never felt good enough for her family and this was one thing she could do. I get her motivation, but she never asked me. Obviously, you never want to invest all your money in the same place. Even her mother didn't invest that much.

"Turns out brother-in-law had gotten mixed up with some shady people. She lost everything, but never told me. Not even when it was on the news. Not when he was arrested. When he was set to go to trial about six months later, I came home and found her in tears. She suffered from depression and tears were common, but she sat me down and confessed that she had gotten notice that our house was being foreclosed on because she hadn't paid the mortgage in months. Then she told me the truth about investing all our money and that we had lost everything.

"I was upset. Stormed out of the house to think. Digest it. Figure out what the hell we were going to do. Once I calmed down, I realized she was scammed by her family. It didn't excuse what she did, but I understood why she did it. I went back and told her it would be okay. That somehow I'd make it okay."

"Did you know how to make it okay?"

"Not really, but I knew my family would help. A week later, I was working on getting the foreclosure stopped when she called me at the office and told me she had sent the girls to my parents' house for the evening. That we needed a night alone."

He stops speaking, a pained faraway look filling his eyes. He closes them tightly and shakes his head, willing some memory away.

"When I got home, I found her. In the garage. Dead. When she killed herself, part of me went with her. I was a wreck, her parents had the nerve to blame me, and the girls cried and cried because they didn't understand where Mommy went. My parents suggested we let the house go into foreclosure and move in with them. I was too devastated to argue, but it turned out to be a good thing. I don't know what I would have done without them. I've spent the last two years being a dad. When Keatyn offered me the job again, they told me it was time."

"I don't understand how she could leave you and those beautiful girls."

"I can understand why she left me. Maybe I wasn't

a good enough husband. Maybe we never should have gotten married. I don't know. But I cannot for the life of me understand how she could do that to our children. So now you know why I have nothing to offer you."

"Dawson, if you truly believe that money is what's important to me, we probably should call it quits. But I think you know love is all you need in life."

"I already learned that love is all you need, Vanessa. That's why I quit work and spent two years with my daughters. They were more important than my pride, than money, than anything. I just didn't know if you knew. Especially when I saw all your jewels."

"I'm sorry if I made you feel like you weren't enough."

He slides a small box out of his pocket and gives it to me.

I hold the box in my hand. It's the size of a ring box. If I were with Bam, I would open it and be dazzled by another jeweled bauble.

I flip the top open to find a dainty, hand-stamped silver necklace—a delicate butterfly whose carved wings form an infinity symbol.

"I know it's not much," he says softly, "but the butterfly symbolizes rebirth and new beginnings, and the infinity symbol—"

"Means we'll be together forever," I finish.

"Mostly, it reminded me of us." He taps the center of the design with his finger. "We started out here and went on separate paths, but both ended up back here in the middle. I hope our paths don't separate again."

"It's the most special thing anyone's ever given me.

Will you help me put it on?" I ask, tears welling up in my eyes.

I stand in front of his mirror.

Put my hand over it.

Press it into my chest.

Then turn and look at him.

The corner of his mouth is turned up, like he's not sure if he should smile yet.

I kiss him, still holding the necklace against my chest.

"I'll cherish this forever, Dawson, and I have no intention of our paths parting. I want to stay right here in the middle."

He kisses me again. Then traces the infinity sign. "How about this time, we go down the same path together?"

Tears fall down my face as he holds my hand and kisses it.

"I love you," I tell him.

"I love you too."

"This is all I want. Your love. Your heart. Your faithfulness."

"That's good," he says with a chuckle. "Because that's about all I have to give."

"Do you know that out of all the jewels and gifts that Bam has bought me, there's never been a reason. Never a story behind what motivated him to buy it. Your thoughtfulness and the meaning behind this necklace make it worth more than any jewel I own."

SHELBY'S BUNGALOW - SUNSET BLVD.

I'M SITTING AT the bar eating dessert and plotting.

I just know Riley is at Keatyn's vineyard for the weekend.

And I'm almost positive that the preppy bitch is going to be there with him.

And, more than likely, they are talking about their future. Based on the snippets I heard, I'm guessing she hurt him and he's not over it but he still loves her.

But if he does, why has he been fucking me all week?

All I know is that I can't let her get in my way.

Somehow, I need to find out more about this Ariela girl. Who she is, how they met, where the hell she came from, and how to get her to go back.

A handsome man sits down at the bar next to me, *accidentally* brushing my thigh with his. Men think they are subtle, but they really aren't. I've seen him staring at me from across the room for most of the night—as are most of the men in the bar.

I'm dressed to kill, had my hair blown out, and am ignoring everyone but the bartender.

Which makes me a mystery.

I put a spoonful of chocolate mousse in my mouth, close my eyes, and savor it, making a contented sigh. The mousse here is so good eating it is practically a religious experience. I know the guy is watching me and thinking he'd like to make me that happy in bed.

And I just might take him up on it. He's wearing a suit with an expensive sheen, a watch that cost more than my apartment building, and a large diamond pinkie ring. When he speaks to the bartender, he has a vague European—or Spanish, maybe—accent. He's not big like Riley, but he oozes wealth and culture.

And there is nothing wrong with a girl having a plan B.

"I'd offer to buy you a drink, but I'm thinking chocolate may be the way to your heart," he says, pointing toward my empty dish.

"Are you trying to win my heart?" I ask, playing coy.

He takes my hand in his. "I like women who believe in living life to its fullest."

"By eating dessert?"

"You, my love, were not simply eating. You were allowing the chocolate to pleasure you. I found myself wishing I were made of mousse. Would you care to join me in my suite where we could pursue the endeavor in private?"

"That's a nice offer, but I don't even know your name," I reply, even though I fully intend to go anywhere this man wants.

He brings my hand to his lips and says, "My name is Juan Fabio Martinez, but my friends call me Bam."

"And what do you do, Bam?"

"Whatever you would like, my dear."

SATURDAY, OCTOBER 18TH
ASHER VINEYARDS - SONOMA COUNTY
Vanessa

I WAKE UP curled into Dawson's arms. I feel a little bad that we didn't go back out last night and join our friends, but I know they will understand.

I kiss his neck to wake him up.

"Morning," he says, his voice gravelly.

"Last night was so incredible. I love you."

"I love you too. Having you know everything makes me feel like a huge weight has been lifted off my shoulders."

"Our past relationships have definitely taken their toll on us. Here's to new beginnings." I give him a sweet kiss since we don't have drinks to toast with. "Are you ready to get up?"

He pushes against me. "I think I'm already *up*."

I slide my hand down his hard torso and discover that he is correct. "Well, I'm sure my bridesmaid's duties can wait a little longer."

"*A lot* longer," he says, rolling on top of me.

163

"You take the word *cock*iness to a whole new level," I tease.

"Damn right, I do."

LATER, WE JOIN everyone in the kitchen where a wonderful brunch is laid out. I'm filling up my plate when Keatyn tosses a printout in front of me. "Hopefully we get through this wedding without helicopters flying overhead trying to take photos."

"Do you think we should tent everything? Is Ariela prepared for that?"

"I am," Ariela says as she walks by and grabs a warm chocolate croissant. "I have them on standby in case it rains. Why, what's up?"

I pick up the article and read it aloud.

"The Life of Keatyn Douglas

"Well, people. Things continue to get juicier in the Keatyn Douglas—Aiden Arrington—Knox Daniels love triangle.

A source tells me that designers are rush shipping wedding dresses straight off the runway to Keatyn's long-time stylist, even though Keatyn's publicist told reporters the actress was planning a Spring wedding.

You all know I was the first to call her pregnancy.

Now, it's safe to say a wedding is in the works.

Keatyn is definitely knocked up and planning a quickie wedding before she announces her pregnancy to the public.

But the question is, who will she walk down the aisle with? Long-time lover, Knox Daniels or her high school sweetheart, Aiden Arrington?

Since we all want to know the answer to that, just for you, I've been scouring interviews and calling in favors.

"The facts as I know them:

1. Knox just purchased property in Sonoma County, close to a certain vineyard.

2. In a recent interview, Keatyn mentioned the Trinity cast has three weeks off before filming in locations around the world.

3. Keatyn recently purchased a swanky, six-bedroom Chelsea abode in London.

4. Knox is packing up and shipping his personal belongings to the above Chelsea address.

The obvious conclusion is that Knox and Keatyn are moving into the London home together to raise their love child.

But sources close to Keatyn say that her relationship with Aiden is stronger than ever.

Could it be that Aiden and Keatyn will get married even though Knox is her baby daddy?

Or is it the other way around?

Did Knox buy a place close to Keatyn because he and his soon-to-be bride need to be close to Aiden, the real baby's father. Or does Keatyn even know who the father is?

Only time will tell, and we won't have to wait long.

Expect a press release announcing Keatyn's elopement and pregnancy in the next two weeks. We're scouring the world trying to figure out where the wedding of the century will be taking place.

One thing is for sure.

She's going to break someone's heart.

And I volunteer as tribute to console whichever man it may be.

Newsflash

Just as I was about to post this article, I got an interesting text. It seems that Captive Films held a special board meeting yesterday where, in an odd turn of events, Keatyn handed over the reins of the company to CEO Riley Johnson by naming him Chairman of the Board. Riley's first order of business was to announce the sale of Captive Films to Front Door Films. There were no further details regarding the sale.

Of course, this wasn't enough information for me, so I went to a top-secret source for details. Here's the word inside Captive.

Employees were shocked to learn about the sale, which was announced Friday after the special session of the board. Apparently the mood was pretty sour until envelopes were handed out to employees, showing the amount of money they would each earn based on their employee stock options, which will soon be fully vested. I'm told cheers of joy erupted, and the offices were then closed for the day to allow for celebration.

Now, the fact that Keatyn is pregnant and

cashing out is not really that big of a surprise. It makes sense that one of the hardest working women in Hollywood would want to slow down.

But here's where things get interesting.

After talking to a source inside Front Door Films, I've learned about a few special concessions to the deal. Keatyn, who famously took over the former A Breath Behind You Films from her stalker, the late Vincent Sharpe, took less money in order to hold on to the Captive Films name. The Daddy's Angel *project along with all of Keatyn's un-optioned scripts were not up for negotiation.*

Then someone mentioned the words Captive North.

With Knox and Keatyn buying up land in Sonoma County, along with her hint recently about the two of them working on a future project, it sounds like L.A. may soon be losing some of its hottest stars to life in the slow lane.

So, Keatyn, inquiring minds want to know.

When are you getting married and to whom?

Call me. Fill me in. Send me an invite!

"*P.S. I'm now totally daydreaming about sitting on a huge front porch with Knox, drinking a crisp Chardonnay and talking about the gorgeous weather.*

P.P.S. Who am I kidding? I'd be sitting on top of him.

P.P.P.S. It may be time to call my realtor.

"Well, I guess the good news is they didn't mention anything about the fundraiser tonight or the fact that the invitations went out so recently. We make it through the next twelve hours, and we'll be golden."

"What do you want to do?" Ariela asks her. "The weather is going to be gorgeous, do you want to put up the tents anyway, just in case?"

She sighs, the thought of her wedding turning into a circus clearly weighing on her. "You know what? I'm going to talk to Knox and have his assistant respond to this woman."

"Don't worry," Knox says, grabbing a piece of Marvel's candied bacon and shoving it in his mouth. "Yum. I can't get enough of this. Have you tried it? Marvel says it's a new recipe. He's wrapping it around chocolate for the cocktail party tonight. Can you even imagine?"

"Knox, why shouldn't we worry?" I ask.

"Oh, yeah. Sorry, got distracted by pork," he says, dishing up at least six pieces of the bacon onto a plate along with more potatoes. "My assistant called me about the article this morning. I told her to take care of it."

"How?"

"Well, Miss Bossy Pants, she's going to let it slip to her source that I *am* moving into the London flat with Keatyn, and that we seem closer than ever. I mean, technically, I am moving in with her. Then there's the fortunate occurrence that took place at the triplets' party."

"What was that?"

"Keatyn didn't wear her engagement ring because it

kept snagging her dress. A different reporter noticed it in the photos from when we arrived and called about it. My assistant told the reporter that at this time she was unable to comment on our relationship status. When the reporter pushed for more information, she told him she could answer off the record."

"What did she tell him?" I ask.

"To expect an exciting announcement on Monday."

Keatyn breaks out into her trademark grin. "Thank you, Knox."

He nudges his shoulder against hers and smiles. "I haven't bought you a wedding gift yet, sugar. So I figured it's the least I could do."

"So, then, no tent necessary, Ariela."

"Awesome, would you like to come see the ceremony site? The altar is up and decorated."

"I'd love to," she says, pulling my hand and dragging me with her. "Vanessa, come with me and see it, then we have to meet Kym and figure out what the heck we are wearing today!"

ASHER VINEYARDS – WEDDING
Keatyn

I'M DRESSED, READY, and counting down the minutes until I get to marry Aiden.

Grandpa comes into my room carrying a large box.

"Vanessa," he says, "would you mind if I have a

169

word alone with my granddaughter?"

"Of course," Vanessa says. "I'll wait outside."

Grandpa sets the box on my bed and sits down next to me.

"You are a vision," he says. "Do you remember when you described your perfect wedding to your grandmother and me a few years ago? And how you imagined wearing a dress with gold embroidery. I see that your dress has just that." He looks down at the sparkly gold Louboutins dangling out from under my dress. "You gonna be able to dance in those skyscraper heels all night, Hotshot?"

"I don't know. They are a little small and already pinching my toes."

"I was hoping you'd say that," he says, patting the box. "This is for you. I had them made right after that conversation and we've been holding on to them for this very day."

"You bought me a present two years ago?"

"Well, I'm not getting any younger. I figured if I kicked the bucket before you two decided to make it official, Grandma could give them to you."

I open the box. Inside are a pair of beautiful light brown leather boots embroidered with gold thread.

"Grandpa, they're beautiful!" I pick one up and examine it closer, noticing that the embroidery isn't just a random design. Mixed into the swirls are symbols of me and Aiden's relationship. There's a four-leaf clover, a Keats quote, a peace sign, an Eiffel tower, our initials, a feather, a moon and stars, and the words bliss, chaos, love, and ifly.

"Grandpa, these boots are like the story of us!" I say

170

as tears fill my eyes. "They are amazing. I'll cherish them forever. And I'm definitely wearing them."

"There's something I want you to know, Keatyn," Grandpa says seriously. "Before he proposed, Aiden asked me for your hand."

"He did?"

"He talked to Tommy as well, but I have to say it choked me up a little—and I don't choke up easily. Grandma says that I'm a ruthless bastard."

I open my mouth to disagree, but he holds up his hand.

"And your grandmother and I made a big decision last night. When we pass, other than a few small bequests and trusts for future generations, you were set to inherit our estate. I don't want to toot my own horn, but your grandpa is pretty loaded. When I bought my farm, the neighbors used to say I was all hat and no cattle, but I showed them. With the sale of Captive, I reckon you really don't need my money, so we've changed our plans. We're endowing our money to the Moon Wish Foundation in the hopes that you and Aiden can do more good things with it."

"Oh, Grandpa—"

"I know. I know. But don't you go getting all teary. You'll make this old man cry, and I can't let Ma see that. She'll think I've lost it and send me to a home."

"She will not," Grandma says from behind us. "Sorry to interrupt, but Ariela says the wedding is about to start, and I have something for you too, sweetheart. When me and this old geezer over here were dating, he didn't have a pot to piss in, but he had big ideas. And although my father told me never to marry a dreamer, I knew your grandfather wasn't just going to dream, he was going to achieve, and I wanted to help him do so."

"Never underestimate the power of a good woman," Grandpa says, "I'm pretty sure I wouldn't have amounted to a hill of beans if it weren't for her. Hell, back then I would've promised anything just to get her to kiss me. Once she did, I realized I'd better deliver."

Grandma rolls her eyes at Grandpa, but she's smiling at him.

"On our first anniversary, we were living in a little shack in Texas near an oil rig, and we didn't have much. To celebrate, he bought a cheap bottle of champagne and this rock, which he told me someday he'd replace with a sapphire. On our ten-year anniversary, he did. I considered giving you that ring to wear today, but decided this old rock has more value, because it represents the promise of love and what you can achieve together." She hands me a smooth blue rock—the kind you find at a tourist stop in different colors. "You should also know that donating to Moon Wish was my idea."

"Thank you, Grandma," I say, giving her a tight hug. "Where do you think I should put it?'

Grandpa holds up the boot. "We had a spot made for it."

Sewn inside the top of the boot is a small suede pouch. Grandma tucks the stone inside, gives me a kiss and says, "I better get going. Your Grandma Stevens and I will be the first up for the processional."

I grab the locket with the photo of my dad and tuck it in with the stone.

Tommy steps into the room, looking handsome in

his tuxedo.

"Are you ready? Ariela says we have to get going now if we want this wedding to start on time."

"Yes, I'm ready," I say, quickly pulling on the boots.

Tommy takes my hands and admires my dress. "You look beautiful."

"Thanks, Tommy."

"I'm honored to be walking down the aisle with you."

"You've treated me like your daughter since you met my mom, I wouldn't have it any other way."

"Then let's go get you hitched," Grandpa says, leading us out the door.

ASHER VINEYARDS - WEDDING

RILEY AND I take our places at the altar. I'm nervous. Excited. Happy. And I can't stop smiling.

I'm standing under an altar decked out in white tulle, softly colored flowers, and a large chandelier—one that Keatyn pulled out of storage, telling Ariela she had purchased it years ago just for this day.

There are ribbons blowing in the trees around us, each hand calligraphed with gold letters spelling out our words of love.

Our favorite quotes from music, poems, and books. Mostly, the books that told the story of our courtship.

Things like: *Top of the Eiffel Tower; A million sunsets; We're sorta like fate; Always. Only. Ever. For you; A piece of cake peace offering; A push-me-over-the-edge-of-the-love-cliff smile; Your lips are my bliss; Hammering. Nailing. Pounding. Screwing; Points for Dances; Panties. I win; ifly; Shh, baby;* and so many others from what she calls the *Swoonworthy List*. A list of all the things I've done—over a thousand of them—that have made her swoon. She says after the wedding is over, she's given the crew strict instructions to carefully take them down and save them because she wants to use them to decorate the ceiling of the nursery, so our baby will live in a cocoon of love.

Her ability to see beauty in everyday life is part of what makes her scripts so good. Even though on the surface most seem like fun romantic comedies, there is always a soulful depth to them that make people fall in love with the story. That is also why the *Trinity* spinoffs with her and Knox have been so wildly successful. Behind all the bombs, danger, and action, she's woven in a tender love story that resonates with everyone.

Especially me.

Our journey to the altar was fraught with danger, action, and heartbreak, but we survived and are stronger because of it.

We've savored every moment we've had together, and I'm looking forward to giving her more *take-her-breath-away* moments. She thinks those moments are things I do to spoil her, but what she doesn't realize is that she takes my breath away on a daily basis. Sometimes when I look at her, I feel like the boy I was when I first saw her—shocked, breathless, mesmerized, intrigued, and completely smitten.

THE GUESTS ARE seated and the wedding processional starts, first with our respective families, our parents, and then her grandmothers who are our flower girls.

The grandmas have huge grins plastered across their faces as they practically dance their way down the aisle, tossing pale pink rose petals mixed with four-leaf clovers onto a metallic linen runner covering the grass.

The two hundred and sixty people here represent the story of our lives—our families, our friends from Eastbrooke, friends from college, teammates from when I played professional soccer, the movie industry, the wine business, and our philanthropic efforts. They are sitting on an assortment of pastel antique furnishings, happily sipping spiked lemonade and still in a bit of a shock from the announcement that the fundraiser was just a ruse to get them here for our wedding.

Vanessa walks down the aisle next, taking her place of honor opposite Riley as the wedding march starts.

Keatyn didn't want to see me before the wedding— a bit of tradition she was adamant about.

I didn't argue.

I mean, we've been lucky so far, and there's no way I'm going to be responsible for screwing that up. I smile broadly as I watch her barreling up the hill in a green, floral-garland-draped Gator utility vehicle. A vehicle that has so much more meaning after learning we conceived after getting caught in the rain—and mud— in one.

When she gets out of the vehicle, my breath catches, the air seemingly sucked out of my lungs by her beauty. She's glowing much like she did the first time I saw her. When I barely believed she could be real.

That's how I still feel today. Like I can barely believe I got so lucky.

A long time ago, she told me about a dream where she was in a meadow, marrying the man she loved. I realize that she's recreated the dream for our wedding as she walks down the aisle wearing a dress etched with gold, her hair in long curls, and a jeweled flower band across her head.

Grandpa Douglas and Tommy stand on each side of her, escorting her down the aisle.

As she gets closer, I feel like *I'm* in a dream.

On one hand, it seems like I've waited so long for this. On the other hand, it feels like only a moment has passed by since the day she kicked a soccer ball at my head.

But today is different.

She wants to be my wife. She's pregnant with my child.

The closer she gets, the more details I notice. The pale roses, pink peonies, and white hydrangeas surrounded by feathers making up her bouquet. The vintage four-leaf clover ring on her finger.

When she joins me at the altar, I tell her she's beautiful.

She doesn't say anything, just looks down. I follow her gaze and watch as she pulls the skirt of her dress up slightly, revealing a pair of cowboy boots and not the gold sparkly heels she had told me she was wearing.

It's then when I'm overcome with emotion.

I swore to Riley that I wouldn't be a pussy and cry,

but it's hard not to get emotional when the person who embodies your life is standing in front of you.

And she's wearing boots.

"You in boots is my favorite," I whisper as I take her hand in mine and kiss it.

ASHER VINEYARDS – WEDDING
Keatyn

I'M STANDING AT the altar looking at my moon boy. My green flash.

His eyes glisten when I show him my boots.

I've been trying not to cry. Not to be all emotional, but when he takes my hand in his and kisses it like freaking prince charming, I feel the tears well up.

And as we face each other to say our vows of love, my heart feels like it could burst with happiness.

"Aiden," I say, stopping to compose myself, then repeating the words he said when he asked me to marry him. "You and I are like a promise. A wish. Proof that luck and fate bring people together. Proof that true love can survive the kiln. I promise to be patient, to continue to build a strong foundation with you, and to live a life unscripted."

His green eyes lock with mine, pulling them in with those tractor beams of his, and making me feel like we're the only two people on the planet.

"Keatyn," he says, "I promise to never pretend punch your head, to watch a million sunsets with you, to love you with everything I am, and to share our love that is utterly, breathtakingly beautiful."

We exchange rings, and the officiant declares us husband and wife.

"I now present to you, Mr. and Mrs. Aiden Arrington."

AFTER WE MAKE our way down the aisle, Aiden and I lead the processional down to the cocktail hour on the brick terrace. Once everyone has gathered, we're pulled aside to go back to the altar to take some photos. I definitely want some as the sun is starting to set.

"You know the tree with our initials carved into it?" he asks me in between smiling for the camera.

"Yeah."

"On our way down to the reception, we need to stop and carve our wedding date in it."

"I love that idea, Aiden."

"So do I get to see these boots?"

"Of course, they're amazing. Like the ribbons in the trees, they are pretty much the story of us. My grandparents had them made."

I pull the skirt of my dress up and show off the boots.

"Wow. They thought of everything. The boots are incredible, just like my wife."

"Your wife. That sounds so cool."

He kisses me. "That's because it is. I realized when I saw you coming down the aisle in a dress with golden embroidery that our wedding was like your dream."

"Yeah, I had such a clear vision of marrying you that day. I couldn't imagine my wedding any other way."

"Well, when you have an epic love story like ours, you had to know everything would turn out perfectly."

"Thanks to Ariela for bringing my vision to life and to Knox. Because of him we didn't have to worry about the paparazzi. By the time we do the press release, we'll be somewhere on our honeymoon. Where are we going again?"

"I haven't told you yet."

"Just a hint, please."

"We're not staying in one location. We'll be moving around."

"Oh," I say, a little disappointed. "I was kind of looking forward to checking in somewhere and relaxing."

"Do you trust me?" he asks, taking my hand.

"Of course, I do."

"Then let's go celebrate."

"I have something I want to give you first," I tell him. "Come in the house for a sec."

We sneak into our bedroom where I have a wrapped present sitting on the bed.

"What is this?"

"Something I've been saving for this day for a really long time."

He rips open the wrapping revealing the bowl I made in ceramics class at Eastbrooke.

"Our love survived the kiln," he says.

"It sure did," I reply, wrapping my arms around his neck and kissing him.

SHELBY'S BUNGALOW - SUNSET BLVD.

Shelby

ALTHOUGH I HAD fun going to Bam's room with him last night, he left town with nothing more than a promise to call me when he comes back.

Needless to say, I'm not holding my breath. Guys *always* say that.

Whatever, I'm bored, and Riley has been gone for long enough. It's time for me to put an end to whatever is going on with my competition and get him back here where he belongs.

While I was lying by the pool and sipping champagne this afternoon, I had a brilliant revelation about Riley. Although he can be swayed by sex, I seem to get what I want more when I appeal to his emotional side.

And that will be the way to get him to marry me— by appealing to his heart.

Now, what can I do to guarantee that Riley hops on that pretty plane of his and gets his ass back to me as fast as he can?

I smile to myself when I come up with the perfect answer.

ASHER VINEYARDS - WEDDING

I'M DANCING WITH Keatyn under the twinkle lights of her reception when I notice a pretty girl with an amazing rack wandering off the dance floor toward the bar.

"Who's the chick in the red dress?"

"That's my friend, Katie. We were on dance team together in high school."

"How is it that I've never met her?"

"I don't know."

"What does she do? And who's the guy with her, her little brother?"

"No, that's her date," she says with a chuckle.

"She run a daycare?" I quip.

"No, but she does tend to date younger guys. She's a teacher."

"I bet she could teach me a thing or two."

"Knox!" Keatyn exclaims and gives me a playful slap on the forearm.

"Is she normal?"

"As in not crazy? Yes, she is. In fact, she's been dying to meet you. She calls you Foxy Knoxy."

"You've been holding out on me?"

"You were in a relationship with makeup girl and then were dating Jennifer."

"That's over."

"I heard. Thank you for handling it well."

"She's been flirting with your friend, Troy."

"Aww, really? They'd be cute together. The actress and the world-famous DJ and rockstar."

"Oh, look, the kid just went to the bar. You need to introduce me." I grab Keatyn by the elbow and lead her off the dance floor to where Katie is standing alone.

"Katie," Keatyn says, "I want you to meet Knox. It's hard to believe that two of my best friends have yet to meet."

Katie doesn't say a word, just has her mouth open, staring at me.

"Hi," I say, trying to make her feel comfortable. I mean, I'm used to women getting flustered around me. I am Knox Daniels, after all.

When she doesn't reply to my greeting, Keatyn says, "Katie has a question for you, Knox. One she doesn't understand why no reporter has ever asked you."

"No, I don't!" Katie snaps, her eyes getting big and looking embarrassed as Aiden whisks Keatyn back out on the dance floor. Oh, Katie, don't be shy with Knox.

"Aww, come on. Tell me," I encourage, suddenly feeling desperate to know the question. Katie has a shy, fresh-faced, girl-next-door look on a killer, curvaceous body—just my type.

She flashes a glare in Keatyn's direction then slams her drink, takes a deep breath, and says to me, "Fine. You know how your character in *Trinity* is known for his lip biting?"

"Yes," I say, curious as to where this is going.

"I wondered if you yourself use that technique."

I react by giving her a long kiss, nipping her lip to

end it and expecting her to fall into bed with me. "So, what do you think?"

She frowns. Why is she frowning? I'm an amazing kisser.

"That was nice and all, but it's not what I meant."

Shit. Now I feel stupid for kissing her.

Her demeanor changes from shy and innocent to bold and daring as she puts her hand on her hip, smirks, and leans closer to me.

"What I really wondered is if you do it when you kiss somewhere *lower*."

Now I'm the one with my mouth hanging open.

Just for a minute.

Oh, I like this girl.

I recover quickly. "Well, sugar, would you like to find out?"

She glances at her date who is back on the dance floor grinding on a group of women.

I wave a thumb in his direction. "How old is he?"

"He's legal." She laughs. "Actually, he's twenty-two."

"That's pretty young."

"You're one to talk. How much younger is Jennifer than you?"

"Keatyn said you always date younger guys? Why?"

"I suppose because they're readily available."

"How are they in bed?"

"Hmm," she says, adorably chewing on her lip while she thinks. "I'd say younger guys, like him, are good for fun and intensity, but not big on finesse."

"Finesse? Like lip biting?"

"Like lip biting."

We stare at each other intently, the threat of what we both want filling us with desire. Time to make my move. "Would you like to take a walk with me?"

"To where?"

"Where are you staying?"

"With Logan and Maggie. Here at the vineyard."

"And the boy toy is staying with you?"

"Yes."

"Hmm." I drag her outside then push her up against the side of the barn and kiss her.

Hard.

It's a long, hot kiss.

"Come to my room with me now?" I practically beg. And Knox doesn't beg. But I can't help it. I want her. Now. And although I've never done what she asked if I do, now it's all I can think about doing.

"Um, as much as I'd like to, Knox, I can't. It wouldn't be right of me. Kevin and I aren't serious, but it would be really rude of me to just ditch him. I'm sorry."

When she turns and walks back to the barn, I chase after her.

"Wait. Can I call you? Get your number?" When's the last time I had to ask for a girl's number? Middle school? I feel the butterflies I felt back then. Afraid she will say no.

But she smiles at me and pats the front of my suit jacket, totally turning me on.

"You have a phone?" she asks.

"Jacket pocket," I reply.

She retrieves my phone and presses a bunch of buttons.

"I added myself as a contact and sent a text to my number. I have to go, Knox," she says wistfully. "I'll text you back."

Once she's back inside the barn, I check my phone to make sure she actually did what she said.

I can't help but smile when I see the text she sent herself from my phone.

> **Me:** *You're an idiot for walking away from Knox Daniels.*

An incoming text pops up causing me to laugh at her name.

> **Bite Me:** *Don't I know it.*

With a grin plastered across my face, I text her back, deciding to go for it.

> **Me:** *I have a few weeks off after the wedding and was thinking about taking a vacation. Would you be interested in joining me?*
> **Bite Me:** *I would be, but I have to work. Parent-teacher conferences are this week. Although, I do have Friday off.*
> **Me:** *Where do you live?*
> **Bite Me:** *Cincinnati.*
> **Me:** *I've always wanted to visit, but I bet it would be really tough to get a hotel room on such short notice.*
> **Bite Me:** *Is that your way of asking if you can stay at my place?*
> **Me:** *Do you have a spare bedroom? A couch I can crash on?*
> **Bite Me:** *Knox Daniels, you know damn well that if you come to my house you won't sleep on the couch.*

At least not alone.

Me: *Are you going to use me and throw me away like your boy toys?*

Bite Me: *It all depends on how good you are.*

Me: *Oh, sugar. I'm the definition of good.*

Bite Me: *Every guy thinks that. You'll have to prove it.*

Me: *If I do, will you go away with me for the week-end?*

Bite Me: *Yes. I will.*

Me: *Where shall we go? Fiji? Milan? Paris?*

Bite Me: *Those places are amazing, but far away. We'd waste the whole weekend traveling.*

Me: *We wouldn't want that. You choose. Anywhere you want.*

Bite Me: *IF you prove it, don't laugh, but I've always wanted to go to Washington D.C. and see all the museums.*

Me: *Then that's where we'll go. I love museums.*

Bite Me: *Really?*

Me: *I'd love going to a museum with you. Maybe I'll learn a thing or two.*

Bite Me: *Well, I am a teacher.*

ASHER VINEYARDS – WEDDING
Keatyn

AFTER AN AMAZING meal followed by numerous toasts, everyone is back out on the dance floor.

I'm trying to find my husband in the crowd when

186

Aiden's voice comes over a microphone.

"If I can have everyone's attention, I have a little surprise for my bride. We shared our first kiss at a school carnival, and I'll never forget how she looked. She was wearing a little red dress and was eating pink cotton candy."

"With me!" Riley yells out.

"And me!" Dallas adds.

Aiden laughs. "That is true, but luckily I whisked her away to the Ferris wheel. It was at the top of it that we shared a perfect first kiss."

Aiden sets down the microphone and stalks toward me.

He grabs my hand and says, "Now, please."

And I'm thinking *now what* until a pathway is revealed, lit up by twinkle lights. We walk down the path, which leads us around the barn—where there's a Ferris wheel.

"Ohmigosh, Aiden! It's beautiful."

"Want to go for a ride with me?"

"Uh, yeah."

As we're getting ready to board the first car, I notice gold scrolling letters on the pale pink paint.

Keatyn and Aiden

October 18th

We're sorta like fate.

"Did you buy this?"

Aiden grins. "I did. It's my wedding gift to you. I had it completely restored. Thought it would be a good addition to the farm."

"Our kids will love it. It's beautiful," I say, getting

on the ride.

As we approach the top, I squeeze his hand. "You know, I have to admit when I first fell for you, it was because you were so hot, Mr. Shirtless Goalie." I pat his stomach. "You're still pretty sexy looking, but you're so much more than that, Aiden. You're so wonderful to me. I'm so incredibly lucky." I start to cry.

"Don't cry, baby," he says as I lean my head against his shoulder, just like the first time we rode the Ferris wheel together.

When we get to the top, it feels like time stops again.

Especially when he presses his lips into mine.

"I've died and gone to hottie heaven," I say, teasing him.

"That's because I just gave you a slow, perfect, time-stood-still, fireworks-in-your eyes kind of kiss," he teases back.

"You're stealing my lines."

"There's a reason for that," he says, as fireworks light up the sky.

"Fireworks. You think of everything," I tell him. "I love you."

"I love you too, Boots."

As we watch the fireworks, I can't help but remember when he lit up the sky for me in a different way. When he put hundreds of glow-in-the-dark stars all over my ceiling.

And I know now is the right time to tell him.

WHEN THE FIREWORKS show is over, and the Ferris wheel starts moving again, I say, "Top of the Eiffel

Tower. Top of the Ferris wheel. Top of the hill overlooking the ocean. All special places to us. Places where our lives have changed."

"And now we're officially hitched."

"Always. Only. Ever."

"Now you're stealing my lines," he jokes. "Just like you did the night you told me you're pregnant."

"And the night you proposed. I have something I need to tell you, Aiden. When I went to the doctor on Monday, they did an ultrasound because my hormone levels were off."

Panic fills his eyes. "Is the baby alright?"

"Yes, but I found out that there's not just one baby. There are three. We're having triplets."

"Triplets?" he repeats slowly.

Then he leans over the seat, causing it to rock unsteadily as he yells down to the crowd. "TRIPLETS, EVERYONE! WE'RE HAVING TRIPLETS!"

"Well butter my butt and call me a biscuit. Did you hear that, Ma?" Grandpa says from the car above us just as Aiden's mother screeches, "Triplets?!"

The crowd below us murmurs with excitement over the news.

"Well, I guess the cat's out of the bag. Holy shit, Aiden! You just told the world I'm pregnant!"

He pulls me close and kisses me again, leaving me breathless and not caring about anything other than his lips.

"When Inga read your palm during high school, she was wrong," he says.

"She told me I'd have twins, then two single pregnancies. Very close together."

"Twin boys, a girl, and then another boy."

189

"Maybe the triplets are two boys and a girl. Wouldn't that be amazing?"

"As long as they're healthy," he says, sliding his hand across my belly in wonder and shaking his head in disbelief. "Triplets."

ASHER VINEYARDS – WEDDING

"TRIPLETS," I SAY to Dallas, shaking my head. "How crazy is that?"

"It's pretty crazy," Ariela says from behind me.

I turn around and face her. "The wedding has been incredible. You did an amazing job. Keatyn couldn't be happier."

"And what about you?"

"Logan told me that making this wedding perfect wasn't just for Keatyn—that you wanted to show all of us that you were sorry."

"Mostly you," she says softly. "My duties are officially done for the night. Would you like to dance, Riley?"

"I would," I reply, pulling her into my arms and swaying to the music.

"So tonight's supposed to be the big night," she says, looking grim. "But I meant what I said about us not needing to decide anything yet."

"Let's go talk somewhere in private," I say, leading her off the dance floor and stopping to grab some champagne on the way to my room.

After popping the bottle and pouring us each a glass, I get to the matter at hand.

"Explain why you didn't send me the letter. I need to understand why you didn't fight for us."

She sits on the bed, crossing her legs into a pretzel, just like she used to when we would sit on my bed and talk and kiss for hours at a time in high school.

"I cried most of the way home. As we were pulling into our driveway, my dad finally spoke. He asked me if I told you. I said yes, and that's when I noticed I was still clutching the note in my hand. I told my dad that I had written you a letter but forgot to give it to you, so he asked what I was going to do with it. If I would send it. I checked my phone for the millionth time, but upon seeing nothing from you, I told him that I didn't know what I was going to do, but that I was surprised you hadn't called or texted me. My dad smiled and said that the reason you hadn't is because he was right. That you didn't care about me. I decided I would keep the note on my desk for three days, and if I hadn't heard from you, I would throw it away and try to forget about you."

"But you didn't," I state.

"No, I couldn't do either. That's what I don't think you understand, Riley. You weren't the only one who was devastated."

"You're right. I shouldn't have given up. I should have called and texted and stalked your house."

"I kept praying for some kind of sign. What I should have been praying for was strength. I should have been strong enough to call you myself. I just want you to know how sorry I am. I was young, and scared, and foolish then, but I'm not anymore. I want to be with you, Riley. And I'm not afraid to say it. I still love you."

I reach out and touch her cheek, caressing it. "And I still love you."

"It's not going to be easy, Riley. I still have to get a divorce. But I want you to know that I will spend the rest of my life trying to make it up to you."

"I don't want that," I tell her, causing a frown to form.

"I see," she says softly, looking ready to burst into tears.

"I want us on a level playing field, Ariela. We were supposed to decide today if we want to go forward. If we want to date. What do you want?"

"You, Riley. Just you. Actually, that's not true. I want to marry you, have babies with you, and love you until you're old and gray."

"That's all I've ever wanted, too," I say as her lips land on mine. "And I think it's about time we let ourselves be happy."

She hugs me and then rests her head on my shoulder, causing me to feel like I've stepped back in time.

"I want to be happy," she says.

"You know, maybe it wasn't meant to be back then. Over the last ten years, I've worked long crazy hours to make the company what it is. I gave it my life. Now we're selling it and I can now reap the rewards. I'm getting my life back. And I want to spend that life with you, Kitty."

"I want that too," she says, pushing her lips against mine and ripping off my clothing as quickly as she can.

We're naked, lying on the bed, making love when

my phone rings.

And then rings again.

And again.

"Uh, I better check that," I say, reluctantly pulling out.

"Who is it?" she asks as I look at my phone.

"Shelby. I'm going to call her back."

Ariela frowns but nods in agreement as I make the call.

"Riley!" Shelby cries into my ear. "I was robbed. Mugged! A man put a gun to my head and told me to give him my new Fendi baguette. I told him no, so he punched me in the stomach and took it anyway. Now I'm having cramps, and I'm afraid I'm going to lose our baby, Riley. I don't know what to do. Please, don't make me go through this alone. Please come home."

Even though the girl of my dreams is lying naked in front of me, I know I'm being pulled in a different direction. My child's mother needs me.

"I'll be there as fast as I can," I tell Shelby, grabbing my clothes and quickly getting dressed.

"Where are you going? What's wrong?" Ariela asks.

"Shelby got mugged. Punched in the stomach. She's cramping."

"Is she in the hospital?"

"I don't know. I think she's at the hotel."

"Riley, it's not unusual for pregnant women to cramp from time to time. And honestly, if she's cramping and losing the baby, there isn't much you can do about it. Why don't you stay the night and go home in the morning?"

"The mother of my child was fucking mugged, Ariela. Sorry, but I have to go."

About the Author

Jillian is a *USA TODAY* bestselling author who writes fun romances with characters her readers fall in love with, from the boy next door in the *That Boy* trilogy to the daughter of a famous actress in *The Keatyn Chronicles* to a kick-ass young assassin in the *Spy Girl* series.

She lives in a small Florida beach town, is married to her college sweetheart, has two grown children, and two Labrador Retrievers named Cali and Camber. When she's not working, she likes to travel, paint, shop for shoes, watch football, and go to the beach.

Check out Jillian's website at www.jilliandodd.net for added content and to sign up for her newsletter.

Made in the USA
Coppell, TX
08 February 2020

15609595R10115